By the Skin of His Teeth

Also by Ann Walsh

Beginnings: Stories of Canada's Past (editor, 2001)
The Doctor's Apprentice (1998)
*Winds Through Time: An Anthology of Canadian Historical
Young Adult Fiction* (editor, 1998)
Shabash! (1994)
The Ghost of Soda Creek (1990)
Moses, Me and Murder: A Story of the Cariboo Gold Rush (1988)
Your Time, My Time (1984)

By the Skin of His Teeth

A Barkerville Mystery

Ann Walsh

A SANDCASTLE BOOK
A MEMBER OF THE DUNDURN GROUP
TORONTO

Editor: Michael Carroll
Production and Design: Jen Hamilton
Front Cover Photograph: Copyright © by British Columbia Archives C-07674, "Song" Cook at McKinnon Hotel, Barkerville
Back Cover Photograph: Copyright © by British Columbia Archives F-07769, Barkerville Looking South on Main Street 1868, Richard Maynard
Author Photograph: Lynette Winders Photography
Printer: Marquis

Library and Archives Canada Cataloguing in Publication

Walsh, Ann, 1942-

    By the skin of his teeth / Ann Walsh.
"A Barkerville mystery."

Originally published: Vancouver : Beach Holme Pub., 2004.

ISBN-10: 1-55002-634-8
ISBN-13: 978-1-55002-634-4

    1. Barkerville (B.C.)–History–Juvenile fiction. 2. Chinese–British Columbia–History–Juvenile fiction. 3. Racism–British Columbia–Barkerville–History–Juvenile fiction. I. Title.

PS8595.A585B9 2006   jC813'.54   C2006-901507-4

Conseil des Arts du Canada   **Canada Council for the Arts**   Canadä   ONTARIO ARTS COUNCIL CONSEIL DES ARTS DE L'ONTARIO

We acknowledge the support of the Canada Council for the Arts and the Ontario Arts Council for our publishing program. We also acknowledge the financial support of the Government of Canada through the Book Publishing Industry Development Program and The Association for the Export of Canadian Books, and the Government of Ontario through the Ontario Book Publishers Tax Credit program, and the Ontario Media Development Corporation.

Care has been taken to trace the ownership of copyright material used in this book. The author and the publisher welcome any information enabling them to rectify any references or credits in subsequent editions.

J. Kirk Howard, President

Printed and bound in Canada
www.dundurn.com

Dundurn Press
3 Church Street, Suite 500
Toronto, Ontario, Canada
M5E 1M2

Gazelle Book Services Limited
White Cross Mills
High Town, Lancaster, England
LA1 4XS

Dundurn Press
2250 Military Road
Tonawanda, NY,
U.S.A. 14150

*This book is for "Peter"
and the many Chinese Canadians
who had to fight so hard before they could
finally call Canada home*

Acknowledgements

Thank you to the following people who, by so generously offering their support, encouragement, and expertise, made this book possible: Bill Quackenbush and his staff at the Barkerville Archives; teachers Rumiana Cormack, Joan Anderson, and Niki Ticinovic and their students; the Williams Lake Writers' Support Group; the British Columbia Arts Council; John Walsh, patron of the arts; the Redl Family; Lily Chow; and Rod Hawkins, Crown counsel, Williams Lake, British Columbia.

Author's Note

The racist attitude toward the Chinese that is portrayed in this novel is unfortunately true of that time in Canada's history. The words I have put into the mouths of both the real and fictional characters have been taken from history books, the *Cariboo Sentinel* (Barkerville's newspaper), and the transcript of the trial.

The historical characters in the book are Alexander Robertson, Crown counsel; George Walkem, twice premier of British Columbia; Chief Constable James Lindsay, who is buried in Barkerville's cemetery; Judge Henry Crease, whose judicial wig can be seen in the Maritime Museum in Victoria; Sing Kee, whose store is on Barkerville's main street; Moses Delany Washington, Barkerville's barber; Ah Ohn, the primary witness; Dr. J. B. Wilkinson; and, of course, Ah Mow.

One

The wind tore at me. Tiny ice pellets, not quite snow, definitely not rain, stung my face like dozens of angry winter bees. I tightened my woollen scarf, pulling it up almost over my eyes, but the wind ripped it away. I had forgotten to wear gloves. My hands were numb and wooden with cold.

I wrestled with my scarf again, settled my hat farther down around my ears, thrust my hands into my pockets, and kept walking. Twice I lost my footing and nearly fell. The road from Richfield to Barkerville was snow-covered, the wagon ruts frozen, the potholes treacherous crevices where deeper snow tugged at my boots. Another gust of wind slapped at my scarf, and once more I tried to adjust it to protect my face. As I wrapped it high on my cheeks, I realized that some of the ice pellets on my skin must have melted. Even my numb fingers could feel the moisture under my eyes.

Surely these aren't tears? I am sixteen, and a man my age does not cry.

I walked through silence along the Cariboo Road. Williams Creek, so noisy in summer as it tumbled over its

gravel bed, was muted by a layer of ice. Many of the miners'
claims that clustered between the creek and the road were
deserted now, the cabins dark and empty under their thick
caps of snow. Only a few brave miners continued their search
for gold through the Cariboo's bitter winter. Most left the
gold fields, returning with the robins months later, full of
hope that this time their claims would yield pay dirt or even
the mother lode. Today, November 3, 1870, I was alone on
the road. I walked in silence as thick as the snow, silence that
was broken only by the howl of the wind and the occasional
crack of a snow-laden branch as it snapped.

"*Murder!*"

The shout ripped through the icy air. I stopped, stilled by
fright. But all was quiet again. *Perhaps I dream,* I thought.
Perhaps the nightmares that once plagued me so badly have returned.

"Murder!" The cry came again.

I looked behind me up the road. No one was there. The
road below was also empty—no human form, no ghost.
Nothing.

Then other voices and a woman's high-pitched scream
echoed up from the town. This was no nightmare, I realized.
Those were real voices I was hearing, troubled frightened
ones. Shaking off the fear that had kept me motionless, I
began to run, slowly at first, then faster, past Stout's Gulch,
past the entrance to Billy Barker's Never Sweat Claim, and
finally into the town itself.

People filled the street, blocking my way. I stood at the
edge of the crowd, wondering what had happened. It was still
early, but it seemed as if most of the inhabitants of
Chinatown were not only up and about this morning, but

were gathered here.

The throng surged noisily forward. I moved with it, not understanding what was being said. I spoke no Cantonese, and here, in this part of Barkerville, only a few spoke English. But the voices seemed angry, maybe afraid.

Someone called my name. "Master Ted."

It was Sing Kee, the herbalist. "There is trouble, Ted. Please come with me."

"What's happened?" I asked. "What's wrong?"

He pulled me through the crowd. "Let us pass, please," he said, switching to Cantonese. I recognized my name, "Theodore MacIntosh." Then Sing Kee said loudly in English, "Dr. Ted will help."

I wasn't a doctor. Once I was a doctor's apprentice, but the fire that nearly destroyed Barkerville two years earlier also ended my hope of becoming a physician. Sing Kee knew very well I wasn't a doctor. He also knew his knowledge of medicine was far greater than mine. If someone were hurt, Sing Kee would know what to do. Why was he insisting I could help?

He must have sensed my confusion, for he leaned close to me and whispered, "A bad thing has happened, Ted, very bad. My people are upset."

"But what can I do?"

"Look around you. There is no other white man here but him, the evil one. You must help."

"How?"

"Speak with strength. Try to bring calm."

We had reached the front of the gathering, and I saw, lying perfectly still on the steps of a restaurant, a Chinese man. His eyes were open and he stared straight ahead. There was blood, much blood. It was on his face, on his clothes, splashed onto the wall behind him. I tried not to look, but couldn't help myself. I turned to Sing Kee. "This man is—"

"Yes, he is dead. And the man who killed him is white."

"I don't understand..." I began.

"Please, Ted, help us. My people trust you. They trust you, but they are angry at the white man who killed Ah Mow. You must stop the trouble before it spreads."

I didn't really understand, but Sing Kee is my friend. I did what he asked.

"I have medical knowledge. Let me through," I said with more confidence than I felt. The crowd parted and grew silent.

Even if Sing Kee hadn't told me the man's name, I would have recognized the still figure. He was Ah Mow, the owner of the restaurant on whose steps he was sprawled. "Allow me to examine him," I said.

I had only been a doctor's apprentice for a few short months, but even to someone with no medical knowledge, it was obvious that Ah Mow was dead. There was a large wound on his chest from a knife, I thought. I bent over the man and listened for breath. There was none. I felt for the pulse of blood in his throat. There was none.

Gently I shut the dead man's eyes and stood to face the gathering. "I can do nothing for him."

"That man, he is the murderer," Sing Kee said. "Many saw." He pointed at a tall white man in the centre of a circle of Chinese.

"Mr. Tremblay," I said, recognizing the prisoner.

He grinned at me over the shoulders of those who restrained him. *"Bonjour, Monsieur MacIntosh."*

"Sir, you are accused of murder," I said. "Is this true?"

"Murder? *Moi?* I do not know, Ted. Who cares?" He grunted and doubled over, as if he had been hit in the stomach.

"Don't harm him," I said quickly to the Chinese men around him, hoping they would listen. "The law will take care of Henri Tremblay. If he's committed this murder, he'll be punished."

Sing Kee translated my words. A restless wave of sound swept through the group. I thought I heard bitter laughter, but that didn't seem reasonable. What was there to laugh at when I spoke of justice?

"We must send for the chief constable at once," I said loudly over the noise. "He'll question Mr. Tremblay and any who saw what happened. The law will make sure the truth is discovered. Justice will be done."

"I have already sent someone to fetch..." began Sing Kee, but Henri Tremblay's guffaw interrupted him.

"Incredible!" the Frenchman said. "You will send for the *law*, Monsieur Ted? *Pourquoi?* Why disturb the chief constable? It was only a Chinaman, a Celestial. What matters the death of one of them?"

Two

Ah Mow was only one of many who had died in Barkerville. Death was a frequent visitor to the gold fields where the work was hard, the winters harsh, and diseases sometimes seemed to hover over the town as thickly as the black flies did in the summer heat.

Death wasn't unusual in my town, but murder was.

I was glad to see Chief Constable Lindsay when he finally arrived. Although I stayed by the dead man's side, the mob had become unruly. I hadn't been sure how long I could keep the men from seriously injuring Mr. Tremblay. Anger surged around him, and though he laughed and shouted curses, I could see that his bravado was failing, that he was afraid.

The chief constable dismissed me with thanks and took over the unpleasant job of dealing with Ah Mow's body. So I left to continue the errand that had brought me to town early this November morning.

Two hours later I was ready to begin my day's work. But before I went to the carpentry shop I walked farther up the road to where Ah Mow had died. I stood for a moment outside his restaurant, staring at the dark stains on the stairs, then began to retrace my steps toward Pa's carpentry shop. Just past the restaurant was a small building known as the Tai Ping Fong, or Peace House. It was here that ill or dying Chinese men were taken. Others in their community tended to them, bringing them food and medicine, staying with them until they recovered or death claimed them.

Although much of Barkerville had been destroyed in the great fire in September 1868, today no signs of the devastation could be seen. Most of the lower town had been completely rebuilt, and the fire had spared the buildings in the community's upper end. The tiny Tai Ping Fong, like most of the buildings of Chinatown, had survived the blaze.

There was a young woman in front of the Peace House. Even though I saw only her back, draped in a long green shawl, I recognized her. That was Bridget's shawl.

She worked at the Hotel de France, and more than a year ago she had been my close companion during a difficult time. It was Bridget who had comforted me, as I her, when together we mourned the death of a friend.

"Bridget!" I called, "Oh, Bridget, I'm pleased you're here."

She turned toward me, but it wasn't Bridget.

Confused, I blurted out, "Excuse me. I thought you were Brid...I thought you were someone else."

She smiled. "Nae, do not apologize, sir. It was not a glaikit mistake at all."

"Excuse me?" I said again, this time because I didn't understood what she had said.

"It is not glaikit, or foolish, at all to mistake me for Bridget. I am her cousin Jenny, newly arrived from Scotland to live in this wild country. Although I have only been here a short while, many have mistaken us for each other, even though I am *much* younger than my cousin."

Jenny wore a bonnet, and her hair was tucked under it, but a few unruly blond curls had escaped and lay against her cheeks. Her hair was a soft gold, while Bridget's was brown. Except for the colour of her hair, she looked a lot like a smaller, younger Bridget. But when she spoke she didn't sound at all like Bridget. She had brought Scotland with her in her voice.

I glanced at her feet. They were encased in thick boots that made them appear clumsy. She followed my eyes. "This country of yours is cold, sir. My cousin lent me a warm shawl and a pair of her boots. They're a mite too large for my feet, but they'll suffice for now. I do fear my clothes are nae so stylish as those I wore at home. I see few stores here that carry fashionable garments for women, though Mr. Moses's barbershop seems to be well stocked with ribbons, lace, and leather gloves."

"I'm pleased to meet you, Miss Jenny. My name is—" I began. But she carried on as if I hadn't spoken.

"Have you heard, sir? There was a murder just a few steps up the street this very morning!"

"Ah...yes, I've heard."

"This Barkerville is a dreadful town. Why, there was another murder here not so long ago. The murderer was hanged on the evidence of a barber who recognized an oddly shaped gold nugget that had belonged to the dead man."

"I recall that incident well."

"The streets of this town seem paved with violence. Well, since they're nae paved at all, just snowy, rutted paths not like the streets of Inverness, which are real streets—"

"How long have you been here, Miss Jenny?" I asked, trying

to change the subject.

"A mere two days, sir. I was thankful to end the long journey. Would you believe it, a small satchel—a *very* small satchel—was all I was permitted to take aboard the ship that brought me to this country. How on earth a woman is expected to clothe herself adequately with only the contents of one small suitcase—well, it's very difficult. The boots I had with me were nae suited to this climate, and I lost my good shawl on the boat from Victoria to New Westminster. It was a long, cold stagecoach journey up the Cariboo Road without it, I assure you. Bridget lent me some of her clothes until I can find more suitable attire."

For some reason I felt myself blushing. "F-forgive me," I stammered. "You have much the same manners—and looks—as Bridget, though now that I see your face there is...I mean, I know Bridget well...I mean, she's a friend...I mean, she was a good friend of a friend of mine...I mean..." What was wrong with my tongue? I wondered. It wouldn't behave, and the words it struggled with made little sense. But Jenny seemed not to have noticed.

"Mistaking me for Bridget is easily done, sir," she said, smiling. "Don't be distressed by your error. Indeed, I'm pleased that so many in this town know my cousin. I hope I, too, will find friends here." The smile changed her face, making her resemblance to Bridget no longer so striking.

I finally found my tongue. "Welcome to the gold fields, Miss Jenny. I'm a friend of Bridget's and—"

"You've been crying. Is all well with you?"

"Crying? Me. No, not at all. It's the wind."

She stared at me silently.

"The wind, yes, it's only the wind that's made my eyes water," I repeated.

"Oh, the wind, was it? I see." She looked as if she didn't believe me, but then she turned again to gaze at the small building in front of her. "Perhaps you can tell me, sir. This wee building—is it the one the Chinese people call the Peace House?"

"Yes," I said, relieved she had changed the subject. "Tai Ping Fong is the Chinese name."

Her nose wrinkled, and she looked puzzled. Hers was a very small nose, slightly turned up at the end. "To be sure this place is so ordinary that I'm disappointed. I would have thought it would be bigger and more grand." She wrapped herself tighter in the thick woollen shawl and shuddered. "Who would believe that such a dreadful thing happened here?"

"Pardon?"

"My cousin wrote to me of it. She told me that a young boy, scarcely older than I, kept vigil here with a dying man. Bridget says this boy nearly lost his own life here. It was a miracle that he was rescued from the deadly fumes of the great fire. My cousin believes it was the ghost of the hanged man who saved the lad."

Ghost? I did not want to speak of ghosts. I took a breath, wondering how I should answer. But I didn't have to say anything, because Jenny went right on talking.

"He was most brave, don't you think, sir? This boy. Although he will have grown by now, as I have. But he was very young—it happened more than two years ago—when he sat here alone and comforted a dying man. He would have been afraid, don't you think?"

I swallowed hard, my urge to introduce myself vanishing.

"My cousin says I must be sure to meet this young man," she continued, unaware of my silence. "He was to be a doctor, but when the fire came he knew he was needed elsewhere, so he took work as a carpenter and helped to rebuild the town. Do you know of whom I speak?"

I swallowed again but managed to say, "Yes," my voice threatening to squeak on even that little word.

"Ah, you're fortunate. He must be a very courageous person, for when he was even younger he helped to arrest the man who committed that other murder I spoke of. Oh, but you know of that evil deed."

"Yes," I said, my voice higher than normal. "Yes, I do. Very well."

"Only twelve was this lad, so Bridget says, when he bravely pointed out the murderer who would have escaped had it not been for—"

"I'm afraid I'm late for work," I interrupted. "Forgive me, I must go." Jenny had her mouth open to ask me—or to tell me—something else, but I bowed and made my escape, almost running down the street, heading for Pa's shop.

I took a quick look behind me. She was staring after me, hands on her hips, mouth open as if about to call me back. Or as if she were going to chastise me for my rudeness in leaving so abruptly. Perhaps it was my imagination, but I thought she stamped one sturdily booted foot as she watched me retreat.

Jenny had spoken of bravery. Although anyone would have to be brave to try to carry on a conversation with this

talkative young woman, I would need to be especially courageous the next time I met her.

For I was the "brave" person she spoke of, and right now
I did not feel brave at all.

I had lied to Jenny. I wasn't late for work. My father didn't
expect me at the carpentry shop this morning. I had stayed
away with his permission.

"I can manage without you tomorrow," he had told me
the previous night, "though it will be difficult. You've
become a fine craftsman, and many of my customers now ask
for you when they need a carpentry job done. But on the
anniversary of your friend's death you should spend time
mourning him. Go to the graveyard and honour his memory."

It was hard to believe a year had passed since Dr. John
Wilkinson had died. I had always called him "J.B.," not "doctor"
or "Mr. Wilkinson," and for a short time I had been his
apprentice. And, like Bridget, I had also been his friend.

I missed him greatly, so much so that at times I thought I
heard his voice, or saw him going by on the street or leaning
out the window of the stagecoach. Once I ran after a man,
shouting, "J.B., it is you!" The stranger turned, puzzled. I
muttered some excuse, my face red with embarrassment, my
eyes prickling with unshed tears.

His grave was marked only by a simple wooden cross. Less
than an hour earlier I had knelt beside it, shivering in the bitter cold. "I miss you, my friend," I said. "I miss you, J.B."

I had planned on going to the Wake Up Jake restaurant to

have something to eat before heading to work, but now I wasn't hungry. Perhaps Pa would close the shop for a while and come eat with me later when my appetite returned. Of course, Pa didn't like eating in restaurants. He said it was foolish to spend good money on food that could be brought from home for much less cost. So maybe I would eat alone. It didn't matter. I wasn't hungry.

My father glanced up when I came into the carpentry shop, but he didn't say anything. I began to explain about the murder, but he already knew.

"I heard," he said. "But you have work to do. We'll talk later." Our carpentry shop was only a short distance from Ah Mow's restaurant, and gossip travelled quickly through Barkerville's streets.

I added wood to the stove and placed a pot of glue on top of it. A rocking chair, a fine piece from England, lay dismantled on my work bench. The dry air of Cariboo country had shrunk the glue holding the chair together, turning it into a dry powder that no longer kept the rocker intact. I had promised the chair's owner that it would be as good as new by tomorrow, and now would have to work quickly to keep my promise.

It was nearly lunchtime when a knock on the door startled us both. Pa called, "Come in."

Chief Constable Lindsay blew into the shop. "It's bitter for so early in November," he said, wrestling to close the door against a gust of icy wind. "The winter may be a long and harsh one."

My mother maintained that *all* winters in Barkerville were long and harsh. Many miners and storekeepers left the Cariboo for the milder climate of the coastal areas, but my family stayed winter after winter, struggling to keep the path to the outhouse cleared of snow, waking several times during the night to stoke the wood stove, braving the ice-covered road on every journey to town.

Most of the time I liked being in Barkerville through the winter. Even though many of the stores were closed and shuttered tightly, the homes and businesses that remained open were always decorated for the Christmas season. In December lamps glowed softly against evergreens wreathed around windows, and lace tablecloths and silver candlesticks graced tables. If the weather wasn't too bitter, the Cariboo Glee Club would go carolling. There would be sleigh rides, with warm drinks, good food, and dancing afterward. Since so few people stayed in town, those that remained grew closer in friendship. There were many dinner parties, dances, and literary evenings to while away the long, dark winter nights.

Like us, the chief constable spent the winter in the gold fields, for crime is no respecter of seasons.

"What's happened?" I asked. "Has Mr. Tremblay been arrested?"

"Unfortunately I did have to arrest him, Ted, though it doesn't seem right. He's an upstanding member of our community, and it's a shame that he'll be locked away. However, we'll do our best to keep him comfortable. I had a new mattress brought to the jail, and my wife, a fine cook as you may know, will prepare his meals herself."

"But if he killed Ah Mow—"

"*If*—and that remains to be seen—he did, it's obvious it was self-defence, Ted. You know how those Celestials like to fight, though it's usually among themselves."

I frowned. "There was no weapon near Ah Mow's body, no knife or gun lying beside him. I don't believe he attacked Mr. Tremblay. How could it be self-defence?"

"The jury will decide that, Ted. Don't worry your young head with those details. Perhaps we'll learn more at the inquest."

"The inquest? What's that?"

"The coroner—Dr. Bell—has examined the body, and now he'll tell a jury how Ah Mow died. Those who witnessed the murder, if anyone did, will say what they saw. The jury will decide if the death was accidental or not."

"I see."

"If the coroner's jury finds that Ah Mow met his death at the hands of a person or persons unknown, then we must have a trial and Mr. Tremblay will be subjected to further indignities."

"But if he killed Ah Mow—"

"It's early days to be deciding that, Ted. First the inquest. Come along."

"Me?"

"Of course you. That's why I'm here. I came to ask your father if we could borrow you. Your testimony may be needed. You were there only moments after Ah Mow died."

"I was," I said, remembering fresh blood steaming in the cold. Suddenly I felt hot, and I moved toward the door, opening it and standing in the rush of fresh air that swept into the room.

"What are you thinking of, Ted?" The chief constable moved closer to the stove. "Shut that door, please. I've only recently escaped from the bitter cold and must soon return to it. Just as I'm beginning to thaw my frozen fingers, you fling the door wide and invite winter back in. What's the matter with you?"

Slowly I closed the door, then turned to face him. "I saw nothing that many others didn't also see. There's no need for me to go to the inquest, is there?"

The chief constable laughed. "Many of the Chinese say they saw *everything*. But to get any sense out of those heathens—well, it will be as much as we can do to get a straight story. Besides, everyone knows Celestials would as soon lie as breathe."

"That's not true—" I began, but the chief constable didn't let me finish.

"Put on your coat then, Ted, and let's be off."

"Now? The inquest is *now?*"

"The jury is convened, the coroner is ready to begin. We've delayed the proceedings until your arrival, but everyone is waiting."

I swallowed hard. "But I haven't had lunch," I said, even though I didn't feel at all hungry.

"Lunch must wait on justice. Come along."

Reluctantly I went.

Three

The Theatre Royal, where the inquest was being held, was packed. I took a quick look, but thankfully didn't see Jenny in the crowd. I was relieved. I knew I would have to meet her and be properly introduced sooner or later, but I preferred that it be later. Much later.

In the theatre the curtains were open and a table had been set up on the stage. Dr. Bell sat behind the table, and there was a row of chairs, filled with men, to his left.

Chief Constable Lindsay led me to the front of the theatre. Sing Kee and two other Chinese were there as well as a few other men whose names I didn't know. "Sit down," the chief constable said. "We kept these seats for the witnesses. My, there's quite a crowd. Sit, Ted. You'll have a good view of the proceedings from here."

I sat beside Sing Kee, who nodded at me. "So. You will be a witness. That is good."

This was an excellent seat for watching musical perform-ances, but it wasn't so good when every person behind you was staring at the back of your neck, wondering what you were doing there. At least that was what it felt like to me—as if a thousand pairs of eyes were boring into my neck. I could feel myself, neck and all, growing red.

Mr. Tremblay and another man sat on chairs on the other side of Dr. Bell, and a constable stood behind them. The Frenchman wasn't handcuffed, as far as I could tell, but he didn't look happy. His frown drew his face into deep creases and narrowed his eyes.

"Ah, the helpful boy," Henri Tremblay said when he saw me. "The one who is almost *docteur*." He laughed briefly, then fell silent when the man beside him put a hand on his shoulder.

"This coroner's court is now in session," Dr. Bell said. "The jury has been selected." He motioned to the men sitting on chairs. "The Honourable Mr. Walkem, a fine solicitor, is here to watch the interests of the accused, Mr. Henri Tremblay. Let us begin. Mr. Walkem, I understand you wish to address this inquest."

The man beside Henri Tremblay rose and bowed. "If it please the court, sir," he said, "Mr. Tremblay is well-known in Cariboo as a proprietor of a farm near Quesnel Mouth, the owner of a store in Mosquito Creek, and a dealer in agricultural products. He bears an excellent character and is much respected by the entire community. It is impossible that such a man would commit murder. Arresting him has been a terrible mistake."

"I agree," said Dr. Bell. "It is unfortunate. But as you well know, Mr. Walkem, this is not the time for such remarks. First, we must proceed with the inquest, after which Mr. Tremblay will appear before a magistrate and at that time you may present all the testimony you wish about your client's upstanding character."

Mr. Walkem thanked the doctor and sat again.

I stared at the floor. My stomach felt peculiar, but whether it was from hunger or something else, I didn't know.

A Chinese man was led to the stage, and the jury foreman asked him his name. He was Ah Ohn, he replied, and was on the street when Ah Mow died.

"Are—were—you and Mr. Mow related?" asked the foreman.

"No."

"Then why do you have the same name—Ah?"

"It means like 'mister.' Not real name."

"Oh, now I understand," the foreman said. "So tell us, Mr. Ohn, what did you see?" The audience was completely still; it almost seemed as if no one breathed.

Ah Ohn looked directly at the foreman as he answered. "I see murder. I see white man kill Ah Mow." He pointed at Henri Tremblay.

There was a gasp from the people in the audience. It appeared they found the proceedings just as entertaining as the last performance at the Theatre Royal, a melodrama with an evil, bearded villain and a vain but beautiful heroine.

The coroner waited until everyone was quiet again before he asked, "So you claim you saw murder done, Mr. Ohn? Could you be more specific, please?"

The witness looked at him, not understanding the question.

"More details. Details of what you claim to have seen."

"Details? What is details?"

"Explain what you saw," said the coroner. "Tell us exactly what happened."

"What happen, yes. First I hear, then I see. They shout,

the white man and Ah Mow. I hear noise, so I come out to street. I see white man has knife."

Mr. Walkem rose. "Excuse me, but would it be possible to have this witness identify the type of knife? I have a few examples here, if the witness wouldn't mind taking a look." He gestured at a table where a white cloth covered some objects.

"Of course," answered Dr. Bell. "An excellent idea of yours, Walkem."

The lawyer whisked the cloth away and motioned for the witness to move closer, while the audience members craned their necks to see what was on the table. Some even stood, hoping for a better view. Mr. Walkem picked up a pocketknife, lifting it so that the audience and the witness could see it clearly. "Was the knife you say Mr. Tremblay was holding like this one?"

Ah Ohn shook his head. "Too small."

"Like this one?" the lawyer asked, brandishing a large carving knife with a bone handle. That knife looked very much like the one my father used to carve a roast. I shuddered.

"No, no, too big" was the reply.

"Perhaps more like this," Mr. Walkem said, picking up a third knife. This one was smaller, about eight inches long, and the blade glittered. It must have been newly sharpened. It could have been a hunting knife, but one with a longer blade than most.

"Yes, like that," Ah Ohn said.

"Are you sure it wasn't a clasp knife like this one?" Mr. Walkem reached across the table and picked up a pocketknife.

"I say already that knife too small," the witness answered.

"But this isn't the knife I showed you earlier," Mr.

Walkem said. "*This* knife, this 'too small' knife, is the one Chief Constable Lindsay found in the coat pocket of my client when he arrested him."

This time the audience's reaction was loud, and the coroner glared as he said, "In spite of Mr. Walkem's theatrics, this is a coroner's inquiry, not a dramatic performance. Those in attendance will kindly keep that fact in mind."

Mr. Walkem sat down beside Henri Tremblay. The two men exchanged glances; both looked pleased. But it was the jury foreman who asked the next question. "Where exactly was Mr. Tremblay when you saw him?"

"Beside Ah Mow. He kneels in snow beside Ah Mow. Ah Mow on ground. Ah Mow dead."

"You knew for sure that he was dead?"

"Yes. Much blood."

There *had* been much blood. I, too, had seen it.

"And how do you believe Ah Mow was killed?"

"With a knife," Ah Ohn said. "That man, he kill Ah Mow with knife. Ah Mow holler loud. Ah Mow holler, 'Murder!'"

As if they were one person, everyone in the audience gasped. Then the room grew quiet once again, so silent that it almost seemed as if we could hear the words Henri Tremblay spoke when he leaned toward his lawyer and whispered something in the man's ear.

Mr. Walkem listened for a moment, then stood again. "Did Mr. Mow speak English?"

"Some words," Ah Ohn said. "Not much."

"So how is it that a man who speaks very little English has the presence of mind to shout 'Murder' in a language that isn't his own tongue?"

Ah Ohn looked confused once again.

"Why did Mr. Mow shout in *English?*" Mr. Walkem repeated.

"To make white men hear," Ah Ohn said, finally understanding. "Ah Mow want help from constable. So he use English word."

"Oh," Mr. Walkem said, looking disappointed. "Where were you when you *say* you saw Mr. Tremblay kneeling beside Mr. Mow?"

"Two, maybe three doors away. Nine, ten feet. I see clearly."

"Did you?" said Mr. Walkem. "You saw clearly? Are you sure about that?" But before Ah Ohn could answer, the lawyer turned away. "No further questions for this witness."

Another Chinese man was called to testify. He didn't speak English, so Sing Kee translated for him. His story was much the same as Ah Ohn's. He had heard men shouting and had come out of his house to see what was happening. He had heard Ah Mow cry out. He had seen Mr. Tremblay kneeling beside the murdered man.

The doctor who examined the body was summoned next, and he gave his report. It was long, and I couldn't concentrate on what was being said. A shuffling and restlessness in the audience made me take notice just as a sentence describing the injury, "a wound at the scapular end of the clavicle dividing the subclavicle artery," was read. I realized that not many in the audience understood the medical words. Most of the terms the doctor was using I knew from my days as Dr. Wilkinson's apprentice, but even I was mystified by *scapular* and *clavicle* until Dr. Bell pointed to his own chest, showing everyone the exact spot of the injury.

"The wound was severe," the doctor explained. "Severe

enough to probably cause instantaneous death."

Then Dr. Bell called my name. "Theodore MacIntosh, are you in attendance?"

Swallowing hard, I said, "Here, sir," and stood.

"Young man, your name has been presented by Mr. Sing Kee as a possible witness, though Mr. Walkem, appearing for the defence, informs me you'll have nothing to add to these proceedings. Were you, in fact, present when this murder took place?"

"No, sir." I swallowed again. "I came later, after—"

"I understand that you stayed with the body until Chief Constable Lindsay arrived. Is that correct?" Mr. Walkem asked, coming to the edge of the stage and peering down at me as he asked the question. In his black robes he looked like a large raven inspecting the ground, searching for something to eat.

I tried hard not to feel like a plump and nourishing worm as I answered, "Yes, sir."

"And you saw my client there?"

"Yes, sir."

"Was he near the body?"

"No, sir. The body—uh, Mr. Mow—was on the steps in front of his restaurant. Mr. Tremblay was in the middle of the road."

"Were you close enough to him to see Mr. Tremblay's face?"

"Yes, sir."

"And was there blood on his face? On his coat? Or perhaps on his hands?"

"No, sir. I saw no blood."

"Do you not find it odd that a man who has been accused of murder had not a speck of blood on him only moments after the deed was committed? How do you suppose that was possible?"

"I don't know—" I began.

"Mr. Walkem," Dr. Bell said, "I understand that you have only the best interests of your client at heart, but this is not a trial. This is merely, as I am sure you know well, a coroner's inquest where a jury will determine the cause of death. Please save your arguments and any further questions until the trial—if, in fact, one becomes necessary." He then turned back to me. "Unless you saw the murder happen, Theodore MacIntosh, you are of no use in this inquiry. You may leave, if you wish."

I *did* wish. I wanted desperately to get back to Pa's shop, to get away from all these gawking people. As I made my way out of the theatre, I once more felt their stares on my back.

Just as I pushed through the big front doors I heard the coroner say, "We will now hear the testimony of Chief Constable Lindsay."

But I wasn't hearing Dr. Bell's voice. I was hearing once again the cry that had reached out to me through the cold air as, early this morning, I had made my way down the Richfield road.

Murder! Murder!

Four

The wind was still blowing, lifting the morning's new snow from the ground and tossing it into my face. I pulled my scarf tighter as I walked to Wake Up Jake's. I would have something to eat, I thought, perhaps even a cup of coffee—though I didn't usually care for that bitter beverage—before I returned to Pa's carpentry shop. I was cold again, as cold as I had been earlier that day on the Richfield road.

As I pushed through the restaurant's door, the rich smell of freshly baked bread made me realize I was truly hungry. I had only eaten a biscuit in the morning before leaving home, and it was now well past two o'clock.

Hanging my hat and scarf on the stand, I found an empty table close to the wood stove. I was about to sit when a cheerful voice from behind me called out, "Ted, Ted, over here. Come and sit with us. I have someone I want you to meet."

I didn't see who it was who called to me, but I didn't have to. I knew that voice. It was Bridget's. I strongly suspected that I didn't want to meet the "someone" she had with her. Reluctantly I turned and slowly began to make my way to the back of the restaurant where two women sat at a small table.

"It's good to see you, Bridget," I said. "And to meet you again, Miss Jenny."

"You two have met?" Bridget asked, puzzled. "Jenny, you didn't tell me you'd already been introduced to Ted MacIntosh."

Jenny's face turned very red. "Nae, we haven't been properly introduced, Cousin. Though if this young man had had the courtesy to identify himself when we spoke earlier today, I would have been saved much embarrassment."

"Forgive me," I said. "But there wasn't time to—"

"You had more than enough time to tell me who you were. There I was, blethering on about your brave deeds and you just standing there not letting on that you were you."

"But I—"

"I don't understand how—" Bridget said at the same time. But even the two of us speaking together were no match for Jenny. She went on talking as if she hadn't heard us.

"Had you but told me he had such red hair, then this wouldn't have happened," she said angrily to her cousin. "Of all the things you wrote to me in your letters, couldn't you have mentioned, even once, his hair?"

Bridget frowned. "His hair?"

"Yes, his hair. Surely you could have told me that."

"But I don't understand why the colour—"

"Oh," Jenny said impatiently, "you don't understand, not at all. If I knew he had red hair, then I would have known that he was he. I mean, that he was him, that he was..." She turned to me. "It was rude of you nae to identify yourself, sir. Very rude."

I bowed. "I apologize, Miss Jenny. I didn't mean to be discourteous. But you talked so...quickly—" and so *much*, I thought

"—that I didn't have time to introduce myself."

"Churlish. That's what it was. Churlish and rude and behaviour not suitable for a gentleman, though it's no wonder there are no gentlemen here in this terrible cold town with its horrid streets and all this wretched snow."

"Jenny, do tell me what Ted has—"

"In truth, Bridget, it will be a pleasure to deal only with bairns rather than with what passes for 'gentlemen' here in the gold fields."

Bairns? I knew that word. It was Scottish for small children, infants. I hadn't realized that Jenny was married, was a mother. She was so young, and I had thought...*bairns?* She had more than *one* child?

I wanted to ask about those children, to find out if I had misunderstood, but I couldn't form the words. How did I ask such a thing? I stared at Bridget and her cousin, wondering why I felt so unsettled by the news of Jenny's married state. And of her babies.

Jenny continued talking, but I wasn't listening, even though it was hard *not* to listen, for she talked loudly. She was still angry at me, and now everyone in the restaurant knew just how much.

Bridget sighed, then reached across the table to take her cousin's hand. "Jenny, Jenny, dear, do be quiet for one moment and let Ted explain. You're as cross as a hen who has lost her only egg to the farmer's wife, and your face is almost the same colour as Ted's hair. It's not ladylike."

"I have every right to be crabbit, Bridget," she said. "I shall also be angry if I wish to be. Besides, I don't care to behave like a proper lady in front of *him*!" She turned her attention to her bowl of baked beans, ignoring both me and Bridget. In the silent restaurant I could hear the clank of dishes, the scrape of spoons across bowls. No one spoke, and I wondered if everyone had been listening to our conversation.

"Ted," Bridget asked, "what on earth have you done to upset my little cousin so badly? To make her so 'crabbit' as she says?"

"Nothing at all," I said.

"Nothing? Nothing? How can you say that when you—" Her food forgotten, Jenny stood and pushed her chair back so vigorously that it nearly fell over. Her head tossed in agitation so much that her curls bounced. I took a step backward for, though she was shorter than I was and was of slight build, she seemed incensed enough to throw a punch or two in my direction. This small young lady appeared more dangerous than any other woman I had ever met. Not that I was afraid of her, not at all. It was just that I didn't know what I would do if she attacked me. It would be most awkward to run away, but...

I took a few more steps backward, but now Bridget, too, stood. She put her arms around her younger cousin and held her close. "Hush now, little Jenny. Whatever's happened, I'm sure Ted can put it right. You know you're quick to fly into a rage, sometimes with no good reason. Ted is a close friend of mine. For my sake, please, sit down, be calm, and tell me what's upset you so. I'm sure Ted will explain if you quiet yourself long enough to listen. Please, Jenny. For me? I'm afraid that today I have little patience with your temper." Her voice trailed away, and the two cousins embraced, neither one speaking.

After what seemed to me to be a long time, Jenny slowly nodded. Then, in a small voice, most unlike the one she had been using, she said, "Perhaps I was too quick to anger, Bridget. Forgive me, for I know how much you grieve, how much you miss your friend, the doctor."

Both women continued to hold each other, and when they separated, I saw that Jenny's face was no longer red and that there were tears on her cousin's cheeks.

Bridget's voice was low when she spoke. "Please, Ted, sit down, join us. It's difficult to believe it's been a year since Dr. Wilkinson died."

"Very hard to believe," I said. "I think of him so often. I went to the cemetery this morning."

"Ah," Jenny said softly to me. "Now I understand *your* tears."

This time I did not deny them.

"I will go to visit his grave this afternoon," Bridget said. "I only wish there were flowers, something I could take."

"I shall come with you, Cousin, if I may," Jenny said. "You wrote to me so often of Dr. Wilkinson that I feel as if I, too, knew him."

"And in my letters did I tell you the colour of *his* hair?" asked Bridget, trying to smile.

"Nae, I don't think so. But you did tell me of his peculiar manner of speaking and how you and he would go dancing. And how much he loved your buttermilk biscuits. Oh, I wish I could have met him, Bridget."

"So do I," Bridget said. "But that can't be. However, allow me to introduce you to another good friend, Ted MacIntosh. Perhaps we can pretend this is the first time the two of you have met, and you can begin all over. Ted, this is my little cousin Jenny. She recently arrived from Inverness, travelling with Mrs. Fraser's mother who has come to visit her first grandchildren. Jenny is to be nursemaid to Mrs. Fraser's twins."

"A nursemaid?" I said. "So you don't have infants of your own?"

"Of course not! Although it seems foolish to pretend that we have never met, I'll play the game to please my cousin. I'm pleased to meet you, Mr. MacIntosh, but yours is a ridiculous suggestion. I am far too young to have children. Indeed I'm not even married—or affianced."

"Please, don't take offence, Miss Jenny," I said quickly. Please do not take offence *again* was what I meant, though.

"Nae, I shall not. But should you not also say that you're pleased to make my acquaintance?"

"Of course. I'm very pleased to meet you."

"Good," Bridget said. "That's settled, and your disagreement forgotten. Now, Ted, sit with us and have something to eat."

"I *am* hungry," I said.

"Ted is often hungry, Jenny, as you'll learn if you spend more time in his company," Bridget explained with a smile in my direction.

"Actually I'm ravenous," I said, pulling out a chair and sitting. "Though earlier today I didn't have much of an appetite."

"*You* not hungry?" Bridget said. "What on earth could have caused that unusual occurrence?"

"A small matter of a murder, I imagine," a voice behind me said.

We all jumped, and I rose hastily to my feet. Mr. Walkem

and Henri Tremblay had come into Wake Up Jake's, unnoticed by the three of us. Now they stood close to our table. It was Mr. Walkem, the lawyer, who had spoken. He bowed toward Bridget and Jenny. "Excuse me, ladies, for speaking of such distasteful matters, but you've no doubt heard of the morning's events."

"Yes," Bridget said. "Yes, we've heard."

The lawyer bowed again. "Distressing for all concerned. Your young friend, Ted MacIntosh, found himself in the middle of an unpleasant scene. No wonder he couldn't eat."

"But the boy has found his appetite again," Henri Tremblay said, staring at me. "The stupid thing he did—taking the side of the Chinamen against me, a white man—is perhaps how he worked up an appetite."

Once more the restaurant fell silent. Not even the clink of a glass disturbed the hush. I didn't know how to answer the Frenchman, or if I should reply at all. I sat down again, praying Mr. Tremblay and his lawyer would leave us alone. But that didn't happen.

"Have you no tongue?" Mr. Tremblay asked. "I remember you speaking freely to your Chinese friends."

"I took no sides," I said. "And now I want to order some food. I don't think I have anything to say to you, sir." My hands were shaking, but my voice stayed calm. I thrust my hands into my pockets, hoping no one would notice the tremors.

"Mr. Walkem," Bridget said, "I believe this man is your client. Was he not just accused of murder?"

Both men nodded. "Ah, the coroner's jury did find that Ah Mow met his death at the hands of a person or persons

31

unknown," said Mr. Walkem. "But though it's unfortunate that my client is to be tried for that deed, it's well-known he's of good character and could never have harmed anyone. It's a terrible mistake, and the stories of those Chinamen who claim to have seen what happened will soon be proved to be blatant lies. Mr. Tremblay is innocent."

"That remains to be seen," I said boldly. Both men glared at me.

"Indeed it does," Mr. Walkem said. "After the inquest, the magistrate said publicly that he regretted the painful duty he had to perform, that of committing Mr. Tremblay for trial at the next sitting of the Supreme Court."

"But there won't be a trial for months, not until a Supreme Court circuit judge comes here again," Bridget said. "So why is a man who is charged with murder allowed to wander the streets? Why isn't he in jail?"

I had wondered the same thing. From the little I knew of the workings of the courts, anyone charged with such a serious offence was usually kept in prison until his trial.

"The magistrate was agreeable to Mr. Tremblay being released on bail," Mr. Walkem said. "I didn't even have to present any character witnesses, as the magistrate himself is well acquainted with Henri and said that he felt it would be a travesty if such an upstanding citizen were to spend months in jail awaiting trial."

"Innocent men shouldn't be locked up," Henri Tremblay muttered. "And I *am* innocent."

"Of course you are," Mr. Walkem said. "Even the chief constable and the magistrate know that."

"*Oui. Je suis innocent,*" repeated Henri Tremblay. "It matters little what the heathens say. Or what a hungry boy who is almost *monsieur le docteur* says." Then he looked directly at me and laughed.

Five

I didn't see Henri Tremblay after that, not for many weeks. People said he had left town for the winter. After a while, talk about him and the murder of Ah Mow ceased.

I was relieved I didn't have to see the Frenchman, or even hear about him. He reminded me of another man who had once laughed at me, cruel laughter that I heard in my nightmares for many years. The other man had been tried as a murderer, as Mr. Tremblay would also be when the judges of the Supreme Court next came to the Cariboo. But since Henri Tremblay's laugh didn't haunt my nightmares, I could almost forget about him.

Besides, I was too busy to worry about the Frenchman. Pa and I were working hard in the carpentry shop. Everyone, it seemed, wanted something built or repaired in time for Christmas. We seldom finished before seven in the evening, even though we both arrived at the shop early in the mornings. Then one bright December afternoon, with the sun sparkling on a fresh snowfall and glittering icicles hanging from the water pipes over the main road, Pa sent me outside. We kept a kettle and teapot in the carpentry shop so we

34

could have a cup of tea with our lunch rather than go to a restaurant for the beverage, but our supply had run out. Pa asked me to go to Mason and Daly's General Store and buy more. Gladly I put on my coat, suddenly realizing that it had been a long time since I had stepped outside during daylight. I resolved to make the errand last as long as I could, to enjoy the sunshine and the clean-smelling air.

I was watching the clerk at Mason and Daly's wrap the loose tea tightly in brown paper when, from behind me, came a child's loud voice.

"Want sweets! Now!"

A second, almost identical voice took up the chorus. "Want sweets now, now!" When I turned and saw the Fraser twins—and Jenny—I wasn't surprised.

Jenny had a wicker shopping basket over one arm, and with her free hand she was desperately trying to keep both boys close to her. But one of them had escaped and was scampering toward the glass display counter where the jars of stick candy were kept. The twins were barely two and half, but they were quite active for their age and had been walking since just after their first birthday. Now it appeared they had also learned to run—quickly.

I set down my parcel and scooped up the child. "Come here, Robert," I said, then looked hard at him. "You *are* Robert, aren't you?"

For a moment he forgot his quest for candy. "Huncle Ted," he said, grinning. "Want sweets, Huncle Ted."

I grinned back, remembering the day he was born. He had been so small, his hands and feet so tiny. I had been one of the first people to hold him, and I was also his godfather—if, in fact, this was Robert.

"Thank you for stopping him," Jenny said. "But that child is nae Robert. That's Andrew."

"Oh," I said. "They're so much alike I can never tell one from the other."

"I have difficulty, too," Jenny said. "Robert, come back here! At once!" Robert had broken free and was making a dash for the pickle barrel.

As Robert disappeared behind the barrel, Andrew began wriggling in my arms. "Down, down," he insisted.

"Not just yet, Andrew," I told him, reaching out in time to grab Robert as he rounded the pickle barrel, heading for the door and freedom. I lifted him up, too.

Now both children squirmed and demanded, "Down, Huncle Ted, down!"

"Not a chance, boys," I said. "I can see it takes two people to handle you in public, so I'll hang on to you tightly while Miss Jenny does her shopping."

"Oh, Ted, would you? Mrs. Fraser has gone to buy new gloves at Mr. Moses's shop, and she asked me to purchase a few things here while she was busy. She would nae have brought the twins—usually they stay at home with me when she does errands—but it's such a fine day and they needed an outing. I was sure I could handle them, but—"

"I'll be glad to help," I said, tightening my grip on the boys. "But perhaps you could hurry. These two are a handful. Or, more accurately, two armfuls."

"I shall be fast," she promised.

I supposed she did try to hurry, but by the time she talked to the clerk about everything and anything, from the weather to the Christmas activities in the Fraser household, to the colour and style of the new dress she was sewing, my arms had grown tired and the children had become even more impatient.

"Down!" they shouted in unison. Four heels thumped hard against my legs. "Down *now!*"

Andrew and Robert were a good size for their age, and their feet were no longer tiny. I grimaced and put the boys on the floor, keeping one of their hands tightly in each of mine. "Miss Jenny, if you've finished shopping, I must get back to work."

"Of course, here I am blethering on. Do forgive me." She grabbed her basket and swept toward the door, seemingly forgetting all about her charges.

"Miss Jenny," I said again, "if you'd be so good as to pick up that small parcel of tea on the counter and carry it for me, I'll be glad to escort you and the twins."

She blushed. "I'm still new at this nursemaid job, Ted," she confessed, taking my parcel. "I would nae *really* have left without the babes, but sometimes I forget I have responsibilities. Please, I'd welcome your assistance. And your company."

I felt myself blush in turn but covered my change in colour by bending and lifting Robert and Andrew into my arms again. "Here, boys, I'll carry you safely across the street if you promise not to wiggle. The snow is pretty, but it's too deep for short legs." Then, as if it were an afterthought, I added, "I welcome your company, too, Jenny."

Mrs. Fraser greeted me with enthusiasm and invited me to attend an evening of song, music, and poetry reading she was planning for the following week. I accepted with pleasure, turned the twins over to their mother and Jenny, smiled my goodbyes, and headed back to Pa's shop.

I was still smiling as I went inside. Pa was busy at his work-bench, but he looked up when I came in. "Well, here you are at last. I stuck my head out the door a wee while ago to see what was keeping you and saw you escorting a young lady across the street. Luckily I also recognized the Fraser twins, or I would have wondered how you became a family man in such a short time."

"Pa!" I said, not amused. "That was Jenny, Bridget's cousin."

"Aye, I know well who she is. Now, Ted, I want to intro-duce you to someone else."

I hadn't noticed that a Chinese boy was standing near the back of the shop. He bowed. "I am pleased to meet you, Master Theodore. I am Peter."

"Peter?" I asked, surprised.

"My Chinese name is difficult for most white people to pronounce, so I have become Peter."

The boy was tall for his age, but his face was rounded with the plumpness young people often have, as I once had not so many years ago. His smile was enormous, and he spoke English better than any Chinese person I had ever met, except perhaps Sing Kee.

"Peter is our new helper," Pa said. "He's Sing Kee's nephew, and a very good worker. I have Mr. Moses's word on that. We can do with an extra hand around here. Just sweep-ing the sawdust away and cutting enough firewood to keep the fire stoked is difficult when we have so much work to fin-ish before Christmas."

"Helper?" I said. My mouth wasn't cooperating today. I

couldn't seem to speak in complete sentences anymore.

"Yes," said Peter, bowing again in my direction. "I am only twelve, but I am a very hard worker, Master Theodore. You will see. And while I work I shall listen to you and your father speak. From your conversations I shall improve my English."

"Your English is excellent," I said, finally recovering my senses. "You have almost no accent, either, though if you listen too hard to my father, you may find yourself acquiring one. His Scottish accent is still as thick as porridge."

"Nae, 'tis not," said my father indignantly.

Quickly I changed the subject. "How did you learn to speak English so well, Peter?"

"My uncle, Sing Kee, began to teach me when I was very small. Mr. Moses also teach me. For two years I help him in barbershop, sweep floor, run errands, and learn many English words."

"I'm sure you did, Peter," Pa said. "Though many of them are probably not fit to be repeated. Some of Mr. Moses's customers have rough mouths."

"Mr. Moses told me which words impolite," Peter said seriously. "Only once did I use a bad one. It was the word—"

"Why do you want to learn so much English, Peter?" I interrupted. "Most of your people manage with just a bare knowledge of our language."

"I was born in this country, sir. I live here. I need to know the language of my country."

"So you don't plan on going back to China?" I asked. "I thought all Chinese dreamed of the day they could return to their homeland."

"This is my homeland," Peter said simply.

"Aye, and you being able to speak good English will also be a great help to your father," Pa added.

I no doubt looked puzzled, so Peter explained. "My father is Mr. Lee. He owns store in Chinatown. Many of his customers are white. He needs someone to speak to them so they can understand, and to understand *them* when they ask for merchandise. He says no one will cheat a man who speaks good English."

"I'm not sure about that," Pa said. "I've known some customers whose English was excellent, but whose morals weren't."

"Perhaps that is so, sir, but it is my father's wish that I learn English well. One day I will work in his store, but he says I am still too young to handle money, so it better for now that I work where I can learn more English. So I first work for Mr. Moses and now for you, and I learn much."

"You certainly have learned a great deal," I said, amazed.

Six

Peter learned more, much more. He was a quick study, and it seemed as if every day he came to work with a new word to try out on us, a question about English grammar, or something he didn't understand.

"Why do people say *skin of teeth?*" he asked one day. "Teeth do not have skin. Should they not say *skin of gums?*"

"Where did you hear that saying?" I asked.

"From lady who say how she slipped on the stairs from the boardwalk and nearly slid under the wheels of the stagecoach coming down the road. 'I escaped being crushed by the skin of my teeth,' she said."

"It means a narrow escape," I told him. "Something that nearly happened."

"So, because there is no skin on teeth, it means there is nothing—only luck—to stop the accident. I see. I think I see."

In spite of my misgivings Peter didn't seem to be acquiring my father's accent. Even though Pa had the same Scottish burr to his words as Jenny did, I found Pa's accent harsh. But when Jenny spoke you could almost hear a gentle breeze sweeping across the heather of the Scottish Highlands.

With Peter's help Pa and I finished all our commissioned jobs well before Christmas, and I found time to attend Mrs. Fraser's evening of song and poetry. Jenny had managed to put the twins to bed early that night, so she sat with me while we listened. The next week the Cariboo Glee Club, of which I was a member when I could find the time to practise, piled onto two sleighs and spent an evening travelling the Cariboo Road from Richfield to Marysville, sharing carols with everyone.

Jenny was released from her duties that evening, and she accompanied me. She wore a blue wool hood lined with silk and carried a matching muff to keep her hands warm. But as we weary carollers returned to Barkerville, she complained that her hands were dreadfully cold. She offered them to me so I could feel how icy they were, and I took them in my own. Suddenly the stars seemed brighter and the cold wind vanished. I felt warm all over, and though I knew I was blushing, it was dark so I didn't think anyone noticed.

After Christmas, winter gripped us harder. The temperature dropped to well below zero, the wind howled, and it seemed that every day brought another foot of snow. Business in the carpentry shop was slow, and near the end of January my father decided to take some time off. "With you and Peter to handle things, I think I can take a wee rest," he said. "The long walk to the carpentry shop each day has become difficult for me. My bones ache, as if the wind cuts right through me."

So I made the trip down the hill alone each morning, my scarf pulled tightly against my throat, my hands deep in my pockets, my nose reddening and dripping as winter slapped me in the face.

I didn't see much of Jenny after Christmas. She and the twins were confined to the shelter of the house during this bitter cold. In truth, not many people ventured out on the streets. And if they did, they hurried to finish their errands so they could return to the warmth of their own fires.

But no matter when I arrived at the shop Peter was there before me. There was always a fire lit and a kettle hot, and he made me a cup of tea the moment I came in the door. Peter kept the shop immaculate, the floor clean, the piles of lumber neatly stacked, the cans of paints and varnishes organized, the glue pot full. I also found that I was enjoying his company, especially since I had so little work to do.

"So," he asked me one day, "you think my English is sufficient, sir?"

"Peter, I've asked you over and over again to call me Ted, not sir. Try to do so."

He grinned. "So, Ted, how is my English coming?"

"It's excellent. I seldom hear you mispronounce a word or use faulty grammar. You should be very proud of what you've accomplished."

He looked unhappy. "Oh, I am sorry you think so."

"Why are you sorry you speak good English?"

"Because my father thinks it is now time for me to go to work for him. He says I speak English so well that no Chinese person can understand me anymore, and that if I learn more long words, no English-speaking person will understand me, either. Only yesterday he reminds me of old Chinese saying— 'A wise man is modest in his speech.' I think my father believe I am no longer very modest."

"I'll miss you, Peter. I wish you didn't have to leave." I

43

would also miss coming to work to find a warm fire and a clean shop. Many of the chores Peter now did would once again be mine when he left. I had never been fond of sweeping floors.

"I do not wish to leave here, sir...I mean, Ted. I want to stay. I will, someday, be honoured to work for my father, but..."

I had a sudden inspiration. "Can you read English, Peter?"

"Only a little. I learn some with Mr. Moses, but mostly I do arithmetic. I can add longs sums in my head."

"Perhaps," I said, thinking out loud, "you should learn to read and write English, as well. When you work in your father's store, you'll need to understand invoices, write out bills, and read advertisements of new merchandise so you'll know what to order. I think you should learn to read."

Peter's face lit up. "There is another old Chinese saying— 'Without knowing the weight of words, it is impossible to know the intentions of men.' I think that is how it would be said in English. It means that words are important. I shall remind my father of that saying and also tell him that words that are written are important to learn, same as words that are spoken. You are a wise man, sir...Ted."

I bowed my head and tried to look wise. "Thank you."

Peter took my coat and scarf from the hook on the wall and handed them to me. Then he pulled on his own jacket.

"Where are you—we—going?" I asked, startled.

"To ask my father's permission to stay with you longer so you can teach me."

"*Me* teach you?" I hadn't really thought about who would teach Peter. I had assumed Moses or Pa would be Peter's instructor. But Moses had closed his shop and left the Cariboo, as he always did when the weather became harsher, going to Victoria where the winter was milder. Pa seemed to be enjoying his holiday and showed no signs of coming back to work anytime soon. There was also no school in the gold fields. So who else could be Peter's teacher?

My mother had taught me to read. We still had the books she used. I could do it. I *would* do it.

"Yes," I said. "I'll be your instructor, though I'm not a trained teacher."

"I am not a trained student," he replied. "We shall learn new skills together, yes?"

"Yes," I said. "At any rate, we'll both try."

I locked the shop door and put a sign on it that said WE WILL RETURN SOON, then Peter and I headed up the street toward Chinatown.

Before we reached Peter's father's store, however, I heard my name called. "Master Ted, please come visit for a moment with me. You, too, Nephew. It has been so long since I have seen either of you." Sing Kee stood in the doorway to his shop. He bowed. "Come in, come in, please. I shall make you tea."

I couldn't help shuddering. "I'll be glad to visit with you, Sing Kee, but you know I will never again taste Chinese tea."

"Of course, how could I forget? You had an unfortunate experience with that drink once. But I have hot soup on the stove. That will warm you on this cold day."

Sing Kee's shop was dark, the air filled with the smells of herbs, some in open barrels on the floor, some in wooden boxes on the counters, some hanging in bunches from the rafters. He led us past bins packed with shrivelled mushrooms, dried sea horses, and turtle shells of all sizes. There were many other things I couldn't identify, all of them ingredients for his herbal medicines. Next to a wall of shelves holding glass and pottery jars and bottles, there was a small doorway covered with a curtain. Peter and I had to duck as we were ushered into a room at the back of the store.

Sing Kee laughed. "You have both grown so tall. I remember when you were as young as my nephew, Ted. You were much shorter than he is, I believe."

"I am very tall for my age, Uncle," Peter said. "Very strong worker, too."

"Yes, you are," I said. "Peter's been a great help in the shop, Sing Kee. I enjoy his company."

"That does not surprise me," the herbalist answered. He ladled fragrant soup into small blue-and-white bowls, giving one to each of us. I held the bowl in my hands, welcoming its warmth.

"Sit," Sing Kee said, motioning to two low stools beside the stove. "Sit and tell me about your lives. I hear Peter is to begin work with his father. So you and your father will lose your tall, strong helper, Ted."

"Perhaps not," I said. "I think Peter should stay with us longer and learn to read. He'll need to know—"

I didn't finish the sentence. From behind the curtain came the sound of loud voices speaking Cantonese.

Sing Kee's face grew serious. "Excuse. I am needed." He pushed through the curtain, adjusting it behind him so Peter and I couldn't see into the store.

I heard Sing Kee speaking softly, as if trying to restore

calm, but the other voices became louder, the talking faster, and Sing Kee's voice was lost. "Are those men angry?" I asked Peter. "Should we go and help your uncle?"

Peter had grown very still. He was listening hard. "No," he whispered. "Stay here. Stay quiet."

I looked at him, and he shook his head, placing a finger across his lips, hushing me. "Please, sir," he added.

So I stayed silent and listened as the voices swirled around the shop a few feet from me. I heard Sing Kee speak again. This time his voice, too, was loud. Then there was another burst of noise, followed by Sing Kee's voice again, even louder. After that there was silence.

Peter had grown pale. His hands were trembling, the soup bowl he was clutching threatening to spill. "*Shhh,*" he whispered.

Standing, I crossed over to him, took the soup from his hands, and placed it on a small table with my own bowl. Then I stayed beside him, ready to help him or Sing Kee should my assistance be needed.

The quiet lasted for what seemed like a long time. I heard whispering, then footsteps and the sound of the front door opening and closing. Finally Sing Kee pushed aside the curtain and came back into the room. "They have gone. For now."

"Uncle," Peter asked, "what will happen?"

"I do not know. But you must leave. Quickly."

"But we're going to ask Peter's father for permission—"

"Today is not a good day for you to ask a favour in Chinatown, Ted," Sing Kee said.

"Why not?"

"It does not concern you. Please go away. I will speak to Mr. Lee about Peter working longer in your carpentry shop, but not today. Today we have other things on our minds."

"What things?" I asked.

But Sing Kee wouldn't tell me, and neither would Peter. At least not at first.

Back at the carpentry shop I asked him again. "What's the trouble, Peter? What's happening?"

"It is a Chinese matter, Ted. I must not speak of it."

"But you know what's going on, don't you? You understood what those men in Sing Kee's store were saying. Tell me. Perhaps I can help."

"I do not think so. But thank you, sir...Ted."

"Tell me and let me decide for myself."

"I do not think my uncle would be pleased if I repeated what was said."

"Then I won't mention to Sing Kee that you told me. You look worried, Peter. Sing Kee was worried, too. What's happening?"

Peter eyed the door, as if making sure it was tightly closed. Carefully he put the broom away, leaning it against the wall where it belonged, then took the few shavings he had swept from the floor over to the stove. Lifting the iron cover, he tossed them in. They crackled and sparked, the fire briefly flaring up and lighting his face. I barely heard his words when he spoke.

"It is the Frenchman, and his friends."

For a moment I wasn't sure who he meant. "Frenchman?"

"The one who killed Ah Mow."

"Henri Tremblay? I thought he left town for the winter."

"Only for a while. He owns a store at Mosquito Creek. He was there, but he has come back."

"I didn't know he was in Barkerville. I haven't seen him."
My legs suddenly felt weak, so I pulled out a chair and sat.

"But many Chinese have seen him," Peter said. "Every day.
Mr. Tremblay spends much time in Chinatown—at the
restaurants, the gambling houses. He is always there."

"What's he doing?"

"He talks very loudly so all can hear. He calls the Chinese
liars, and other names. Also he laughs. His friends laugh with
him."

"Why do they laugh?"

"They say that he will never go to jail, that those who saw
him kill Ah Mow will not dare speak against him at the trial."

"Why would the witnesses not repeat what they said at the
inquest?"

"They are afraid of what will happen to them if they tell
the truth."

"Nothing will happen. The law will protect them."

Peter studied me for a long time, his face motionless.
Then he smiled weakly. "Ted, you are a good person, but you
do not understand. Many Chinese do not think Ah Mow will
find justice in the court."

"Of course there will be justice, Peter."

"If you say so, sir...Ted. But the witnesses do not believe
that. They are afraid. The Frenchman and his friends tell
them they will be harmed if they speak the truth."

"Mr. Tremblay is threatening them? He can't do that."

Peter stared at me strangely. "Who tells the Frenchman
what he can do or cannot do? The chief constable does not.
The judge does not. Mr. Tremblay is not even in jail. He
walks the streets and does what he wishes."

"You should report him to the chief constable, Peter."

"Would the chief constable believe? Only Chinese hear the Frenchman say those things. White men think Chinese people lie."

"But—"

"Some Chinese do not want to wait for the trial. They want to take law into their own hands. They say one life calls for another life."

It took me a moment to realize what he meant. "Those men in Sing Kee's store want to *kill* Mr. Tremblay?"

"Yes, but they will not. They promise Sing Kee they will hurt no one. My uncle spoke wisely to them. He say it would be bad for all Chinese if they kill a white man. He say to wait for the court to decide."

"And they agreed?"

"Yes. For now. But they are very angry at the Frenchman."

I thought for a moment. "They have a right to be angry, Peter, but not a right to kill. Maybe I can speak to Mr. Tremblay and ask him to stay away from Chinatown until the trial is over."

What had I just said? My mouth had gone dry when the words pushed their way out. "I *will* talk to him," I said again, swallowing hard as I spoke, as if I wanted to take the words back.

"No, sir...Ted. Thank you, but you must not do that. Perhaps you will be witness at the trial. We need you. You respect Chinese people. You will say truly what you saw, and the judge and the jury will believe you. Besides, the Frenchman and his friends would not listen to you."

No, they wouldn't, I thought, remembering how Henri

Tremblay had laughed when he called me "the boy who is almost *docteur*."

"But we must do something. I'll tell Chief Constable Lindsay. He'll believe me." I stood, bumping against the worktable and knocking over a block of wood. It thumped loudly when it hit the floor, and Peter and I jumped.

"Excuse me, sir...Ted, but if you go to the law, it will not help. It will make things worse. Mr. Tremblay and Chief Constable Lindsay are friends. They play cards, drink together. The chief constable will not believe you, same as he will not believe us."

"The chief constable is a good man—" I began.

"Perhaps so, but he is white and we are Chinese. Please, Ted, do nothing for now. If I hear that trouble is coming, I will tell you. I promise. But you must promise *me* that you will talk to no one."

I considered his request, then said, "Very well...I promise. We'll hope nothing bad happens."

"Perhaps Henri Tremblay will go back to Mosquito Creek," Peter said. "If he will stay there until the trial, then we will not have trouble."

"Let's hope he stays away then," I said.

Seven

January gave way to February, then to March. The snow deepened and icicles clustered along the eaves. Spring showed no signs of making an early appearance. The days were getting longer now, but slowly. I still walked to Barkerville each morning well before sunrise, returning home in thick dark.

My father came back to work, feeling refreshed and rested, which surprised me, for Ma had found much for him to do at home. She had new cupboards in her kitchen, bigger shelves in the pantry and a newly resanded and repainted floor in the parlour as a result of Pa's "holiday."

Business picked up, and suddenly all three of us were working hard. The sounds of hammering and sawing and the smells of glue and varnish filled the carpentry shop once again.

Peter's reading lessons became fewer and fewer, but it didn't matter. I had discovered that he had a good knowledge of the English alphabet and could read simple sentences even before we began our lesson. He was also an amazingly quick learner. During the slow winter weeks when there wasn't much to do, we read together from some of the books Ma had used to teach me, and I made lists of words for him to learn to spell. Before long Peter was taking those books, and others I borrowed from the library, home with him at night. He had become a voracious reader. I didn't think he would ever become good at spelling, though. The English language still puzzled him a lot.

"Why must there be so many words that sound the same but are spelled differently and mean different things?" he asked. "It is hard to learn. *Two* is a number, *to* is 'I go *to* work now,' and *too* means 'much of something'—sometimes. Now you tell me *too* also means *also*. And *hole* is much different from *whole*, but they sound the same when you say them. Why?"

"Aye," Pa said. "It's confusing, lad."

"See? You say *aye* meaning *yes*, but it sounds the same as *I* meaning *me*. Why must English be so difficult?"

Neither Pa nor I could answer that question. It was something I had often wondered myself.

Several times now, on Jenny's day off, I had been invited to the Fraser home for dinner. Afterward, Jenny and I sat in the parlour and talked. I was sorry it was so cold that we couldn't go outside and walk together.

Mrs. Fraser and her husband seemed glad to see me when I visited. So were the twins. So, I think, was Jenny.

Pa had begun to tease me about my "Scottish lassie," and even Ma would frequently ask about her. "As soon as the weather's better, you must bring her for Sunday dinner," she said. "It's a long walk to our home in this cold, but once spring comes I expect to meet this young lady of yours."

"She is not my 'young lady,'" I said. "We're just friends."

"Aye," Pa said, winking at Ma.

"Indeed," Ma said, winking back.

"I shall go outside to chop firewood," I said, making a dignified retreat and hoping the back of my neck wasn't as bright red as I knew my face was.

In March the pussy willows came out. I picked some and brought them to Jenny. She took them graciously but seemed puzzled. "These are sticks," she said.

"No, look more closely. See the buds? They're soft, like a cat's fur."

"Oh, they're tiny pussy willows. Thank you."

She still looked mystified. How could I explain to her that those soft buds meant spring was coming? That they were the first sign that other plants would bloom, that the creek would thaw, the snowbanks melt, that winter *would* end, no matter how long and hard it had been?

My mother always gathered an armful of pussy willows, placing them in vases around the house. "These are nature's promise to those of us who live in this fearful climate," she would say. "The promise that summer won't forget us."

Jenny dipped her head to sniff the branches, then looked up and smiled. "I smell spring. It's been such a long winter—and it's nae over yet—but when I smell these, I can smell spring. Thank you." She stood on tiptoe and kissed me on the cheek.

"Me, too, me, too!" clamoured the Fraser twins.

"Oh, you want a kiss, too?" Jenny teased.

"No. Kittens. Little kittens."

She handed them each a willow branch. "Poor dears. You

want to be outdoors as much as I do. Don't worry. Soon we can go out every day and you can pick your own sticks—or flowers." Then she gasped. "There *will* be flowers, won't there, Ted? Real ones? Flowers *do* grow in this dreich country?"

"Most definitely," I said. "The Cariboo doesn't always look so drab. There are many wildflowers here—golden dandelions, red paintbrush, tiny blue violets, orange tiger lilies, pink lady slippers, purple fireweed, soft white Saskatoon blossoms. Soon you'll have all the flowers you want, Jenny."

"It will never be soon enough. I'm most fearfully tired of winter."

We were all tired of winter, but by April the snow on Barkerville's main street was replaced by deep mud. It froze solid nearly every night, but by mid-afternoon it was thick and gooey, treacherous to foot passengers and horses alike. Between the buildings, however, the heaps of snow that had slid from the steep roofs all winter still reached higher than my head.

People began returning to the gold fields; the stagecoach was full almost every time it pulled up at Barnard's Express office. Moses's barbershop reopened, as did two of the general stores. Restaurants ordered new supplies, miners arrived, stocked up with provisions, and headed out to their claims. Winter's back was broken, and Barkerville seemed to come alive again. More and more people braved the muddy streets to venture outside during the day.

By May we no longer had much frost at night. The piles of snow between the houses were almost gone, and the trees were leafing into a soft green. The mud grew deeper, especially after rain, but when the mud dried it became as hard as rock.

Clumps of dried mud clung everywhere—to boots, to the hems of ladies' skirts, to the bottoms of men's trousers. But the sun shone, the days lengthened, and the robins returned. Spring had finally come.

Jenny and the twins now spent a great deal of time out of the house. "The bairns are so speeritie," she said one day, sighing. "It is as much as I can do to keep them from running off."

"Spirit tea? Is that something to drink, or is it another of your Scottish words?"

She laughed. "Nae to drink, you glaikit boy. It means having much energy."

"Oh, I understand. Yes, the twins are energetic."

"Indeed they are. Sometimes they have so much energy that I become tired. But if they run and play outdoors in the fresh air, then they go to bed early and sleep most soundly. So we spend much time outside these days, though I'm afraid I'll lose one of them. They run quickly, and they like to hide."

After thinking about Jenny and her two speeritie charges, I fashioned a sort of double "leash" for Andrew and Robert—two leather straps that attached around their waists and then to a belt encircling Jenny's waist. My invention was a wonderful success. Jenny did complain that sometimes it seemed as if the boys, if they decided to head in opposite directions, would pull her apart. But she was grateful she could now safely take her charges for walks, without fear of them escaping. The sounds of their running feet, the fast thump of four small boots, followed by the lighter patter of Jenny's feet as she followed—or was dragged—became a familiar sound along the boardwalks. The three of them often moved so quickly that passersby dodged out of their way, ducking into the shelter of doorways.

Although Bridget told me disapprovingly that "tearing about town like a wild animal" wasn't ladylike behaviour and she wished her cousin wouldn't do it, most of the townsfolk enjoyed seeing Jenny and the twins. There were only a few children in Barkerville; most of the miners had left their own families behind when they came to search for gold. So whenever the three young people made their frequent appearances on the streets, they brought smiles to many faces.

At Bridget's urging, though, I suggested to Jenny that perhaps she should try to slow down, to walk rather than run when she and the twins were in public. But she laughed. "I will nae be bothered by what a bunch of nosy glib gabbits say," she said. "If some women have naught better to do but gossip, well, let them. I'm doing nothing wrong."

She didn't have to explain to me what a glib gabbit was. I had met a few of them myself, people who would rather gossip about others than mind their own business.

I went to the Fraser home for dinner regularly now, and afterward Jenny and I strolled together, breathing deeply of the soft air, slapping at the mosquitoes and black flies that, like us, were enjoying the spring weather. Jenny visited the carpentry shop often, sometimes bringing with her fresh biscuits or a slice of cake. Pa was very fond of the little boys and kept a box of wooden scraps for them in a corner of the shop. The children called these their "blocks" and stacked the bits of wood into towers, or built roads and walls with them, while Jenny shared a cup of tea—and, of course, conversation—with us.

"She's a fine lass," my father said, "but she does blether on."

"She does *not* blether, and besides, I like the sound of her voice," I said defensively. "It's like a song."

"Aye, it's musical, granted. But she does use it a great deal."

Much as I cared for Jenny, I had to admit Pa was right.

But I was pleased and surprised to hear Jenny's voice wishing me a happy birthday near the end of May. The day before I had been invited to the twins' third birthday celebration, a noisy party with much laughter, many games, and a great deal of sweet things to eat. Jenny had sung to them, then the twins had sung two songs for all of us to enjoy—or try to, for the boys didn't have Jenny's soft, musical voice—then there had been more games and more to eat.

I hadn't told Jenny that my birthday followed the twins', but perhaps Mrs. Fraser had. The next morning Jenny appeared at the carpentry shop, smiling and carrying a parcel wrapped in brown paper and tied with a bit of plaid ribbon.

"Many happy returns, Ted," she said. Once again she stood on tiptoe and kissed me on the cheek. My father coughed nosily behind his workbench, and I thought I heard Peter giggle. Jenny and I blushed. At least I knew she did, because I could see her face redden, and I felt sure that I, too, had turned scarlet.

"Here, this is for you," she said, thrusting the small parcel into my hands. "I made them myself." Then she turned to Pa and Peter and called, "Good day," before scurrying out.

"So, a kiss for your seventeenth birthday, son? That's a good omen. Though your Scottish lassie is a gallus young lady. Usually it's a man who first kisses his sweetheart, not the other way around."

What means *gallus* please?" Peter asked.

"It means impertinent, forward—cheeky would be a common word for it," Pa said.

"Jenny is *not* cheeky, nor is she my sweetheart," I said. "We are merely friends. Good friends."

"Aye, so you say," said my father. "So you keep on saying."

Jenny's present was a dozen thick shortbreads. They were still warm, and I popped one into my mouth. My father glared at me until I offered him one, too.

"Well, your Jenny may be gallus," he admitted, "but this is as good as the shortbread your mother makes. Though it wouldn't be wise to tell her so." He reached for a second piece.

Peter went home for lunch, and when he returned, his face was serious. "This is my last day with you and your father, Ted. I can no longer work here."

"Why?" I asked. "Has something happened?"

Pa was bent over an unfinished tabletop as he stroked a sanding block across it. He seemed intent on his work. Peter moved closer to me, and when he spoke, his voice was low.

"No, there has been no trouble, not yet. But the Frenchman is here. He went to Mosquito Creek again, but now he has come back. He talks to the Chinese who saw Ah Mow die. All the witnesses."

"What's Henri Tremblay saying to them?"

"I do not know, but they are afraid. More afraid than before."

"Why?"

"I do not know," he repeated. "They say only that Mr. Tremblay and his friends frighten them. One witness says he will leave town and not speak at the trial."

"But he'll have to testify if he's asked. It's the law."

"If he cannot be found, then he cannot speak, can he? He will *not* be found, I am sure of that."

"But what has this to do with leaving us? We need your help, Peter. Pa and I have a great deal of work to be completed, and soon we'll begin on outside jobs. Already we have requests for new outbuildings. We need you here."

"I am needed more in Chinatown," Peter said.

"To do what?"

He looked over at Pa. The regular swish of the sandpaper across the tabletop hadn't stopped. My father wasn't listening to us.

"Some Chinese men think the Frenchman and his friends will make more trouble."

"What kind of trouble?"

"That also I do not know, Ted. But I find out."

"How can *you* find out what Henri Tremblay and his friends are planning?"

"I am to be a spy," he said. "That is the right word, yes? One who listens to secrets?"

"A spy?"

"Yes. My English is good. I understand what the white men talk about. Mr. Tremblay does not speak French much. His friends do not understand that language, so he talks in English. I am to work in the restaurant where they often eat and play cards. I will work there and listen to what they say to each other. I will hear what they plan."

"It could be dangerous, Peter. Be careful."

"I will, sir...Ted."

"The judge will be here any day. Soon there will be a trial and this ugliness will be over. Then you can come back to us."

"Yes. I look forward to that. Please, you will tell your father why I go?"

"Yes. I'll explain. Good luck to you."

"Thank you." Peter solemnly shook my hand, bowed to my father, and strode out of the shop.

But I was wrong. The trial didn't happen soon. By the end of May, there was still no word about when a Supreme Court judge would arrive in the Cariboo. It had been a long time since the Assizes had been held in the gold fields, many months since a judge had been sent to conduct trials here. Henri Tremblay wasn't the only one waiting for justice.

Early in June there was an editorial in the *Cariboo Sentinel*:

When do the judges of the Supreme Court intend to honour Cariboo with their presence? Last year the judge arrived later and left much earlier than usual; this year it was hoped things would be altered. This is shameful neglect, even injustice. Much inconvenience is suffered by prisoners and others, but no heed has been paid and now we are in June and have still no knowledge of when the court will sit. There are three prisoners in jail awaiting trial. True, they are only Heathen Chinese and as long as they are in jail they are out of mischief. But there are also two men out on bail awaiting the pleasure of their Highnesses the Judges of the Supreme Court whose delicate constitutions might be injured by a trip to Cariboo before July.

I read the editorial aloud to my father. "Why must the paper always talk about the Chinese people as 'heathens'?" I asked. "The Chinese were a civilized society hundreds of years ago while the British were still barbarians with blue paint on their faces. It's an impolite term."

"Most people truly believe the Chinese are heathens, son. They don't go to church."

"Not to our churches. But they worship in their own way at the Tong buildings."

"Aye, but they don't worship our God, which means in the eyes of good Christians they *are* heathens. Also, Ted, I think some people don't believe that the Chinese are 'real people,' that they're equal to us...to white people."

"But that's nonsense. You know Sing Kee and Peter. How can they not be 'real' people?"

"I agree with you, son, but it wouldn't be wise of you to argue with others on this point. There are strong feelings about the Chinese here. You might offend customers who would then take their business elsewhere."

"But—" I began, but was interrupted as Jenny, led by the Fraser twins, burst into the shop. She was clutching the same issue of the *Sentinel* I had just read from.

"Oh, Ted, look. There are to be races and fireworks and a big celebration on Dominion Day, July 1. See, here's a list of all the things that are going to happen. Wait, Andrew, I shall unleash you momentarily. Robert, you must stay still if you want me to untie you. Good afternoon, Mr. MacIntosh. What is Dominion Day?"

"July 1, 1867, is when the provinces united to form the Dominion of Canada, Jenny. So we celebrate that event."

She frowned. "But British Columbia is nae a part of that dominion, is it?"

"Not yet," my father said, "but many who live here came from

Canada West, so they brought the celebration with them. Besides, soon we'll join the Dominion. I feel sure of that."

"I see," she said, still looking confused.

"Last Dominion Day I entered the Merchant Race and won," I said.

"Aye, the prize was ten dollars," Pa said. He frowned. "Which my son was reluctant to share with me."

I said nothing. My father and I had disagreed about the prize money. Since it was my legs and energy that had won the race, I felt I was entitled to all the prize money. Pa had pointed out that he was actually the "merchant," the true owner of this shop, which allowed me to enter this particular race. He even deducted the dollar entry fee from my share of the winnings, maintaining that, as he had paid it in the first place, it should be returned to him. However, I was allowed to keep the small silver cup that was also part of the prize.

"Are you entering again, Ted?" Jenny asked.

"Not in the Merchant Race," I said, still disgruntled over the division of the prize money.

"Then which race will you run in?" she asked. "Look, the newspaper says there will be a Sack Race, a Hill Race, a Three-Legged Race, many foot races, and even horse racing. A cannon will be fired down the main street to begin the celebrations, and there will be speeches and singing. It will be a grand day. Robert, no, that is nae to eat."

She dropped the newspaper and rescued a small wood shaving that Robert was about to swallow. He opened his mouth to howl a protest, and Jenny recovered another piece from his mouth. "You'll have a stomach ache if you eat those, as you know full well, you glaikit bairn," she scolded. Then, without taking a breath, she added, "Don't you be foolish like your brother, Andrew. Don't put any in *your* mouth." She had learned that what one twin did, the other often copied.

"Which races will I enter?" I wondered aloud. "I don't know." I had a vision of entering them all, winning them all, and presenting Jenny with an armful of silver cups and ten-dollar bills, while she smiled and once more kissed me on the cheek. Then I shook away the thought. I wasn't a swift runner and had only won the Merchant Race the previous year because most of the other merchants were older than I. "I'll think on it," I finally said.

"Well, I'll enter the Sack Race and the Hop, Skip, and Jump," Jenny said. "I'm light on my feet and good at skipping. I'm sure I can win one of those events. Perhaps I'll also take part in a foot race. After all, I've become a fast runner chasing the twins. Yes, I'll try a foot race, as well."

Pa and I exchanged glances.

"Best tell her, son," he said, crouching on the floor and suddenly becoming very busy helping the twins stack their bits of wood.

"Tell me what?" Jenny asked.

"Pa, please?" I had hoped my father would do it, but he shook his head and kept his back turned. So I knew I had to be the one to give her the news.

"Um, Jenny, you see...well, those races are only for men. Not for girls like you...I mean, women," I added hastily.

Suddenly it grew quiet. Even the twins stopped what they were doing and peered up at Jenny. Pa had his back to her, but I knew he was listening intently, the way people do when they think they hear a thunderstorm approaching. It seemed to me that he bowed his head and hunched his shoulders, almost as if he were expecting rain, not words, to fall.

"Only for whom?" Jenny demanded in a quiet voice. "The races are only for *whom*?"

I gulped. "For men. Or boys who are nearly men."

"I see. So women can come to this dreadful country, cook meals, wash clothes, tend to the bairns, and keep the fires going through the winter nights, but they are nae good enough to run in a silly race?"

"No, it isn't like that—" I began.

"So, no woman at all can enter? Nae a single one?" She took a deep breath and began to speak. Five minutes later, the squirming twins tightly tucked under her arms, their forgotten leashes dangling from her waist, she swept from the store. Jenny had said a great deal in those five minutes, but what I remember most were her final words.

"Men! Why did God create such eejit creatures?"

Eight

It was almost a week before I saw Jenny again. I heard her and the twins as they dashed along the boardwalks—often they would run right outside the carpentry shop—but they didn't come in.

Twice I left what I was working on and casually stepped to the door, opening it only to see her retreating back. Once Robert—or maybe it was Andrew—who was trying to travel in the opposite direction, caught a glimpse of me and yelled, "Huncle Ted! Want to play blocks with Huncle Ted, Jenny!" But she ignored him and continued her rapid progress down the street, dragging the protesting child behind her.

"So, do you think your Scottish lassie will return?" Pa asked me one day.

"Who? Oh, you mean Jenny. Why, I hadn't noticed, but she hasn't visited us lately, has she? We've been so busy I really haven't had time to think about her."

"Aye," my father replied. "So you say, lad. So you *say*."

Yes, that was what I said, but it wasn't what I meant, not at all. I missed her, and I was more than delighted when, a few days later, the thundering feet and laughter halted at the carpentry shop, the door opened, and Jenny and her charges came in.

"Good afternoon, Mr. MacIntosh," she said brightly. "The boys were asking if they might have a wee visit, if you have time."

"We shall always make time for you, lass," Pa said, setting the box of wood scraps in the centre of the floor. "Ted, put the kettle on and we'll have tea."

"Why, Ted, I didn't notice you," Jenny said. "But, no, thank you. I nae have time for tea today." She bent to untie the twins, then straightened, their leashes in her hand, watching them as they gleefully dug into their box of "toys." "But it's a good thing you're here, Ted, for I have a request for you from a new friend of mine."

"Of course, Jenny. I'll be pleased to help any friend of yours. What's her name?"

She smiled. "*His* name is Joseph."

"Oh, I see. Joseph. What's his last name?"

"His last name? Morrison, yes, Morrison."

"Oh," I said again. "I've never heard of him."

"He works with Mr. Fraser at the claim in Lightning Creek. He's newly arrived in the gold fields and as yet knows very few people, which is why he asked me to request a favour of you."

"What is it?"

"He's heard that you won the Merchant Race last Dominion Day, and he begs that you'll do him the honour of being his partner in the Three-Legged Race this year."

"I hadn't planned on entering that event," I said. "Besides, I don't know this Joseph. If our heights are uneven, then we'll be poorly matched for that race. I regret that I must decline." I picked up the sanding block and began to push it vigorously across the cupboard door I was working on.

"Oh, Ted, that saddens me greatly," Jenny said. She came to me and put her hand on my arm. "I thought we were friends, you and I. I believed you'd be glad to help a new friend of mine."

"Of course we're friends, but—"

"It would be a great personal favour, Ted, if you'd agree to partner Joseph. See, here's the dollar he gave me. He'll pay the entire entry fee himself. It will nae cost you a penny. I assure you he's a very swift runner. He's only a tad shorter than you. I know he can match his strides to yours perfectly."

"But I don't want—"

"Please, Ted? Mrs. Fraser has assured me she'll care for the twins that day so I can enjoy the celebrations. I'll be staying to watch the fireworks at night. I would nae enjoy them so much if I were to watch them alone. Perhaps you'd honour me with your company and we can watch them together? After you and Joseph win the Three-Legged Race, of course." She smiled again.

"Well," I said reluctantly, "in that case I'll do it. But how will Joseph and I practise? We'll need to practise together if we're to win."

"Joseph won't return to Barkerville until the morning of the races," Jenny said. "But I'm almost Joseph's height, so I'll practise with you."

"So will you practise with this Joseph, as well?" My voice sounded angry, though I wasn't sure why.

"Don't be cross. I'll only practise with you."

"Oh, well, in that case..." Then I blushed as I thought about what practising the Three-Legged Race with Jenny would entail. "But...but...that wouldn't be fitting. We'd have to tie our legs together."

"Aye, that's what happens in a Three-Legged Race. Or is it different here than at home?"

"No, it's the same. But, Jenny, you can't practise for that race in your skirt."

"Of course not. I'll wear my pantaloons, Ted. They're very respectable, see?" She hiked up her skirt a few inches to show the dainty lace nestled around her boot tops.

"Miss Jenny!" my father said, horrified.

Hastily she dropped her skirt. "Well, nae one will see us practise. We'll be careful."

Pa spoke up, his voice stern. "Miss Jenny, most of the people in this town are amused to watch you running about with the bairns, but they wouldn't be amused if they saw you in your pantaloons with your arm around Ted and your leg tied to his. You will not do this."

"But we could practise up near the graveyard. No one would see us there."

Pa laughed. "In this town someone always sees everything, Miss Jenny. Haven't you learned that yet? You and Ted won't practise together. Is that understood?"

Jenny nodded, disappointed. I, too, was disappointed. Although the idea of practising with Jenny had at first upset me, I had begun to think it would have been... I felt my cheeks grow hot again.

"Pa's right," I said. "But you must promise you won't practise with this Joseph, either."

"Did I not already say I wouldn't?" She sighed. "Well, I'll say it again. I won't practise with Joseph. I promise."

There was a knock on the door, and it swung open. Peter entered, took a deep breath, then greeted us. "Mr. MacIntosh, Miss Jenny, Ted, it is good to see you again. I like sawdust smell better than hot grease."

"It's good to see you, too, Peter," I said. "How's your new job?"

"I do not need to work there now," Peter said. "The Frenchman has again gone to Mosquito Creek, so I come back and help you." He scrutinized the floor as he spoke. It hadn't had a thorough sweeping since he left, and the piles of scrap lumber in the corner were in disarray. "I think it is good that I work here again, yes?"

"Aye," Pa agreed, looking around him as if he, too, were wondering if I had swept the floor at all while Peter had been away.

"A grand idea," Jenny said. She had picked up one of the twins and was trying to brush the sawdust from his clothes. "I don't recall the bairns getting so dirty when you were here to keep the floor clean, Peter."

"I also do carpentry like my father," I said. "I'm not merely a sweeper of floors. We've been very busy."

"I know, sir...Ted. But I think it is good that I am back," Peter said, picking up the broom. "Very good."

"I must go," Jenny said, lifting the other twin and attempting to remove sawdust from his legs and arms. "I thank you for doing this favour, Ted. Oh, I must nae forget. Here is the dollar. You'll make sure that yours and Joseph's names are put down for the race?"

"Yes," I said reluctantly. I still didn't want to run with

Joseph, but I had promised. "I'll pay the entry fee and enter our names."

Jenny smiled. "Thank you, Ted." Then, with the twins securely leashed, she swept out of the store, almost dragging her charges.

The twins didn't go quietly, though. "No go, Jenny!" they protested. Stay here!"

All of us watched her leave. "So," Pa said, grinning, "it seems that perhaps your Scottish lassie has found a new boyfriend."

"She is not *my* lassie. She is free to keep company with anyone, even this Joseph Morrison. I only regret that I let myself be persuaded to enter the race with him."

"But you did promise, son."

"Who is Joseph Morrison?" Peter asked, now busy with the dustpan.

"A perfect stranger," I said. "I don't even know how tall he is."

"How tall?" Peter asked. "Why is that important?"

I explained about the race and how, against my better judgement, I would race with Jenny's new friend.

Peter looked confused. "Three legs race? But two people have four legs. How can you race with only three?"

"Haven't you ever watched the Dominion Day celebrations?" I asked.

"No."

"Oh, it's a foolish race," I said, then explained how each pair of racers stood side by side and tied their centre legs so they had to move together. "It takes practice to be able to pace your strides to those of your partner."

"So each person has one and a half legs to run with, right?"

"Yes," I said, though I had never thought of it exactly that way. But half of three was one and a half, so perhaps Peter was right. "I sincerely wish I hadn't agreed to enter, not with someone I don't even know. I'll have no chance to practise before the race."

"I will practise with you," Peter said. "I run very quickly, but I have never tried to run this way, with only half a leg on one side."

"You?" I looked at him closely. "You *are* almost Jenny's height, and she said that Joseph isn't much taller than she is. You'll do very well as a practice partner, Peter. Thank you."

Who would help Joseph Morrison practise? I wondered. No matter. It would be obvious to everyone watching the race, even to Jenny, that I had worked hard to improve my skill. Everyone would know who was the better runner. Jenny would see who was the better man.

Or, as Peter said, the better one-and-a-half-legged man.

Nine

Peter and I practised almost every day during the next few weeks. After work we headed for a quiet street near the upper end of Chinatown where we could run without worrying about bumping into other people. The two of us soon became used to each other's running style. We were a good team, moving quickly, our bound legs working as one.

"We are not bad," Peter said one day, laughing.

"We're doing very well," I said, panting. "I only wish I could practise with Joseph, as well." We had finished for the day. Soon I would head up the Richfield road toward home and dinner, but I stood with Peter for a while, resting and talking. "How are things?" I asked.

He knew what I meant. "Good. The Frenchman stays away. Maybe in Quesnel Mouth, maybe at Mosquito Creek. Not here. So no one worries."

"I'm relieved to hear that. I've heard the judge will come in July. The trial will be soon, and then it will be over."

"For Ah Mow, yes, it is over," Peter said. "Very much over. But for Henri Tremblay, well, perhaps his time in jail is beginning."

"Unless he is sentenced to death. There was another murder here, Peter. The man found guilty of that crime was hanged."

"I know. My uncle told me. You helped the law then. You made sure that man was punished."

"I didn't do much," I said, hoping he would change the subject.

"That man's name was James Barry. I learn that, sir...Ted. I know you will make sure that Henri Tremblay is punished also, same as James Barry was. It is fate."

"I will do what I can, Peter."

"I know."

"However, I don't think of James Barry anymore," I added, then said goodbye and began the long walk home.

That was true. At least I *tried* not to think of James Barry. The nightmares were gone now, but I had heard his laughter in my dreams long after he was buried. Then, on the day of the great fire when so much of Barkerville was destroyed, I had thought I had seen his ghost.

I had told no one except Bridget that I thought it was James Barry's voice that had awakened me from a deep sleep that day, his voice that had told me to run from the deadly fumes of the fire. I had told no one but Bridget that, for a while, I believed a ghost had saved my life.

It wasn't true, of course. There were no ghosts. Something else must have awakened me, and then I imagined the rest. I hadn't seen a ghost. I was absolutely positive of that. I did not believe in ghosts!

As if it sensed the blackness of my thoughts, the sky also was growing dark. A thunderstorm was coming. It had been on a day much like this—the sky grey, rain threatening, thunder growling in the distance—that it had begun. A stranger had stepped out from behind a tree just around the curve in the road ahead and spoken to me. "We'll have to see what we can do about you," James Barry had said.

That was the first time I had heard him laugh. Later he would say he had a score to settle with me, and then my nightmares would begin. Much later I would be at his trial, would hear the judge sentence him to death. The next day he died on the gallows, and I heard the sounds of his dying.

I shook my head, trying to scatter those memories, and quickened my steps. That time of my life was over. Finished. James Barry was part of my childhood, as were my nightmares of him. There were no ghosts and I no longer had nightmares. I was almost a grown man, and I would not let myself think about James Barry anymore.

Walking faster now, I glanced behind me, sure that someone was watching. But there was no one on the road.

"Be not so glaikit," I told myself sternly, using Jenny's favourite word for *foolish*. However, the feeling that someone was staring, that unseen eyes were peering at me, wouldn't go away.

Again I checked behind me, but the road, often so busy, was deserted. The stagecoach had passed by hours ago, and it seemed everyone else had fled, running to shelter before the approaching storm. The trees were still, not a breath of wind stirring their branches or rustling their leaves. It was as quiet as I had ever known this road to be, except for the thunder that rumbled as the sky grew darker.

When I rounded the curve, I heard a voice. "Who is it?" I called, trying hard to keep my voice from quavering. "Who's there?"

A low croak answered me. A raven was perched at the top of the tree. It cocked its head and stared down at me with beady eyes. That was why I felt as if I were being watched! I *was* being watched, but only by a raven, a corbie as Jenny called them.

"Hello, Mr. Corbie," I said, my voice stronger.

"*Croak*," the bird said again, as if it were answering me. The sound was low, drawn out, as if the bird were human and were speaking from the back of its throat. It almost seemed as if the raven were complaining about something.

I laughed. "Good day to you."

"*Bonjour*," the raven replied. From behind the tree stepped Henri Tremblay.

I swallowed hard. "Good afternoon," I said politely, the words thick in my mouth.

"I wish to speak to you. It is good that we are alone."

"But I don't wish to speak to you, sir. Good day." I began walking faster, ignoring him.

"*Pas si vite!* Not so fast!" He stepped into the road, directly in front of me. "You have been playing with one of your Chinese friends. Running. Laughing. *Beaucoup d'amusement.*"

"I don't see how it is any concern of yours, Mr. Tremblay. Now if you'll let me pass..."

He made no move to stand aside so I could continue up the road. "I think, boy, perhaps that you will run away from town before my trial. This is why you practise to run *très rapidement, non?*"

"I will not run," I said. "If I am called on to testify, then I'll do so. It is my duty."

"*Oui. Mais*...but what will you *say* to the judge? You have many friends who are heathens. Perhaps you will lie like your Chinese friends."

"I will not lie."

"But your friends, they *will* tell many lies about me."

"The witnesses will tell the truth," I said.

"Celestials? *Non.* They lie. Always. It is their nature."

"That's not true. Besides, at a trial everyone must tell the truth. They have to swear to it on the Bible."

He laughed. "What means the Bible to heathens? They swear only on a burnt piece of paper. They mock the Bible. You have not had dealings with Chinamen. You do not know their evil ways."

"They're not—" I began.

"You are a boy. You know nothing." He moved closer, his face only inches from mine. I could smell liquor on his breath, and the seasonings of what he had eaten for lunch— garlic, onions, a sour odour. I stepped back, but he drew nearer again.

"So, you must do what all other white men would do. You will say I harmed no one, that I did not kill the Chinaman."

"I don't know whether or not you did. I saw nothing except Ah Mow's body."

"*Oui.* You saw nothing, *tu comprends?* So you will tell the judge nothing. Make sure you do not forget that." He finally let me push past him. "*Au revoir,* boy who is almost *docteur,*" he called to me. "Remember, you saw nothing. You will say nothing."

By the time I reached home, the rain had begun. It was heavy, and my boots were coated in mud. I scraped them well before I went into the house, as if I were trying to remove all

77

thoughts of Henri Tremblay. I wasn't afraid of him. I would not let myself be afraid.

The next morning I casually asked Peter, "Are you sure Mr. Tremblay isn't here in town?"

He looked at me curiously. "No one sees him. Why do you ask?"

"No reason," I said. I resolved to forget about the Frenchman, not to think about him at all.

It wasn't too hard to forget; there were many other things to keep me occupied. Pa and I were very busy in the shop, working much later in the evening than we usually did. And even though I was often tired after work, Peter and I practised almost every day. Some days I would leave Peter to practise yet again with the Cariboo Glee Club.

Excitement was high in the town; the *Cariboo Sentinel* was full of information about the events that would take place on Dominion Day. Each issue of the newspaper had more information about the celebrations—the cannon would be fired at ten in the morning, then there would be inspirational speakers, then selections would be sung by the Cariboo Glee Club. The sports would start at eleven o'clock and continue throughout the day. At noon a royal salute would be fired, and in the evening there would be a special performance at the Theatre Royal by the Cariboo Dramatic Association. Later in the night there would be a grand illumination with lights and decorations in shop windows, and then there would be the fireworks, which I would watch with Jenny.

The horse races were attracting a lot of attention—and wagering—between friends and neighbours. The competition would be stiff for these events—for the awards were high. The

Cariboo Purse carried with it a prize of fifty dollars, and the Dominion Day Race winner would take away the grand sum of a hundred and fifty dollars. No jockeys were allowed; the owners had to ride their own horses.

The main road was cleaned and gravelled, making sure it would be in good shape for the celebrations. The horse racers were warned severely not to practise on that road. The members of the Dominion Day Street Committee had worked hard and didn't want to clean up after more than the usual horse traffic.

One article in the *Sentinel* made me laugh, for I well remembered the chaos during the past year's foot races. SHUT UP YOUR DOGS FOR THE RACES read the headline. "On previous occasions they have proved an intolerable nuisance," the piece continued. "A serious accident might occur during the races, owing to some of these canine favourites insisting on taking a share in the sport." Last year several of the animals *had* participated, without either paying their entry fee or being invited to race. There had been a great deal of shouting and barking, and contestants, dogs, race officials, and spectators all ended up in an enormous seething mass of legs, heads, and tails that filled the street and boiled up onto the boardwalks.

This year a platform had been built on the main street, draped with branches of evergreens and decorated with scarlet banners and gold maple leaves. The speakers and musicians, as well as some honoured spectators, would view the activities from this high perch. Everything was in the final stages of preparation, and Barkerville was more than ready to celebrate.

Peter and I practised one last time on the evening of June 30. The hopeful winners of the horse races had moved their practice area to the same street where Peter and I raced, so we dodged flying hooves as well as steaming droppings as we ran.

"Enough, sir...Ted," Peter said, stopping to clean his boot. "We have practised enough. You are ready to run. I am ready to stop."

I untied the scarf that bound our legs, agreeing with him. Although Dominion Day was tomorrow and I had heard nothing from Joseph Morrison, Jenny assured me he would be there well before the start of the race.

"He will nae come to town until late the night before," she said. "But I know he's a swift runner. I feel sure the two of you will win."

I wasn't so certain. "Where will I meet him? How will I recognize him?"

"If you'll be at your father's shop, I'll bring him to you. The Three-Legged Race is to take place early in the sports program. I'll make sure Joseph is there just after eleven o'clock."

"I'll be there," I said. "I've been practising hard. I only hope Joseph is as well prepared."

"Do not worry yourself about Joseph," Jenny said. "He will nae let you down."

Ten

The morning of July 1, 1871, dawned clear and bright. Not a cloud threatened to hide the sun's face, the soft breeze carried not a hint of rain. It was a glorious day to celebrate, though it appeared that many had begun festivities the day before. All night long carriages and horses went past our house as people made their way down the hill to the saloons of Barkerville, and the sounds of revelry carried back up the hill until the early-morning hours. Some of the racers would find themselves with headaches today, I thought, wondering hopefully if the others entered in the Three-Legged Race would be among the sufferers.

But I had had a good night's sleep and, well before ten in the morning, I was on the platform with the rest of the Glee Club, waiting. At ten o'clock exactly a cannon was fired, the noise and smoke signalling to all that the ceremonies had started. We all sang "God Save the Queen" and followed with a rousing three cheers for Her Majesty. Then the politicians spoke, but luckily only briefly, and the Glee Club performed. After three loud cheers for the Dominion and much applause, the first of the races was announced.

I left the platform and quickly made my way to Pa's shop, hoping Jenny and Joseph would be on time. The Three-Legged Race was fourth on the program, and I wanted to have a few minutes to instruct Joseph on the best way to adapt his running stride to mine before we actually had to race. I also needed to change into my overalls and work boots. I had worn my good suit for the Glee Club's performance, but my mother had warned me not to race in those clothes.

No one was waiting for me in front of the shop. I looked up the street, then back the other way. "Jenny?" I called. "Joseph?"

No one answered. The street was deserted; everyone in town was watching the events taking place on the main road.

Not knowing what to do, I called again, louder. "Jenny? Miss Jenny?"

The door opened a few inches, and a voice whispered, "In here, Ted. Inside." I pushed the door wide and stepped in, blinking in the dim light.

Bridget stood in the middle of the shop, hands on hips, face flushed. "Were you part of this disgraceful business, Ted? Are you responsible for this?"

"For what?" I asked. "What are you doing here, Bridget? Where's Jenny? Where's Joseph?"

"Take a good look at your Joseph," Bridget said, pointing at the rear wall. A small figure stood there, his back to me, his head bowed. He wore overalls, rolled up several inches, work boots, and a large cap pulled firmly down almost to the back of his neck. Joseph was shorter and much thinner than I had imagined him to be. Well, I would have to take smaller strides when we raced. We would manage.

"Joseph?" I said, relieved he was there. "We must hurry. The race will begin soon."

He turned around, and I could see he had been crying. But what was more important than his tears was the fact that he wasn't Joseph. "He" was Jenny.

"Jenny!"

"Yes, this 'boy' is my idiot cousin," Bridget said. "I hope you had no part in this scheme of hers, Ted. If I hadn't been late for the opening ceremonies, I wouldn't have seen her skulking about as she made her way to your father's shop and wouldn't have found out about this until it was too late. We would all have been disgraced."

"Jenny?" I said again, scarcely hearing Bridget.

Jenny lifted her head. The cap was low over her ears and forehead, but a few tendrils of blond hair had escaped. In truth, she looked nothing at all like a boy. She looked nothing at all like a man, either, even though a very black moustache was crookedly painted on her face.

"Oh, Jenny!" I said.

"Can you say naught but 'Jenny' then?" she said, bursting into tears.

"Crying will do you no good, girl," Bridget said. "Although you'd be crying harder if I hadn't found out about this in time to stop you and Ted from racing together."

"But I wouldn't have—" I began, then wisely closed my mouth. Jenny was so obviously herself, even in men's clothes and with that ridiculous paint on her face, that I would have discovered her deception immediately. I would never have allowed her to race with me. But now didn't seem the right time to mention that.

Bridget paid no attention to me. She spoke only to Jenny, her voice loud and angry. "It's one thing for you to dash around town with the little twin boys, tearing about like a wild thing, though some people have been horrified by that behaviour. But Mrs. Fraser says you tend well to her children and will hear no complaints about you, so I've said nothing. But to appear in public in men's clothes, to enter a man's race—that is shameful. Even Mrs. Fraser couldn't forgive that. You would have been sent back to Scotland, you silly girl."

"But Mrs. Fraser helped me," Jenny said through her tears. "She lent me the clothes—they're Mr. Fraser's—and used bootblack to disguise my face. She said she wished she could—"

"Then Mrs. Fraser is as silly as you are. She might have wild ideas about what women can do, but her husband is not so forgiving. Believe me, you would have lost your job once he found out."

"He wouldn't have found out," Jenny said defiantly, her tears forgotten.

"You think not? Your disguise wouldn't fool a single person. Within minutes word would be all over town. Didn't you think about how Ted's parents would be shamed? Or me? People would blame me for your recklessness, for I try to look after you."

"But it was nae so serious a thing to do, Bridget." Two large tears rolled from Jenny's eyes, sliding down her cheeks and lodging in the thick "moustache."

"You think not? You know I have a responsible position managing the Hotel de France. Didn't you think about *me*, about how I could lose my job, as well? About how I could be hurt by your stupid behaviour?"

Jenny's lower lip trembled when she answered. "Nae one would have blamed you, Bridget."

I wasn't so sure about that. The women of this town could be unforgiving, and it was possible that many of them *would* hold Bridget accountable for Jenny's unladylike behaviour.

Bridget turned to me. "Please, Ted, tell me you knew nothing about this. I suspect you didn't, but I need to hear it from your own lips."

If I told Bridget that Jenny's disguise had been my plan, then perhaps she wouldn't be so cross with her young cousin. If I took the blame, then...

But before I could open my mouth, Jenny spoke up. "Of course, it was nae his idea, Bridget. Don't listen to him if he tells you it was."

"Well, Ted?" asked Bridget. "Did you know what she intended to do?"

"Ah...well...I..."

"I shall nae speak to you ever again if you don't tell her you knew nothing," Jenny said. "You won't take the blame for what I did."

"Well, did you know?" Bridget demanded.

I looked to my right. Jenny scowled, her black "moustache" drooping unevenly down the sides of her mouth. I glanced to my left. Bridget glared at me.

"Tell me the truth," Bridget said.

"Don't you *dare* lie," Jenny said. "I don't need you to protect me."

"I...I..."

I don't like to tell untruths, but I couldn't bear to see Jenny in trouble. Surely Bridget wouldn't be as angry if she thought Jenny entering the race was my idea. But if I did that, if I tried to help, I would lose Jenny's friendship. I knew she meant what she said, that she would never speak to me again if I didn't tell Bridget the truth.

"I'm waiting for your answer," Bridget said.

"I'm waiting, too," Jenny said. "Say something, you glaikit boy."

I tried. But all that came out was "I...uh...I..."

Then Bridget took a deep breath and sighed. "No, Ted, it's all right. You don't need to answer. I know you're fond of my silly cousin and will try to take the blame for this even though that will anger Jenny greatly."

"It will indeed," Jenny said.

"I don't need to hear you say it," Bridget said to me, ignoring Jenny. "From the look on your face when you first saw 'Joseph' and realized who 'he' was, I honestly believe you knew nothing about it."

"Nae, he did not," Jenny insisted. She reached up and pulled off her cap. "I'm sorry, Ted. I thought it was a grand idea."

"Well, it wasn't," Bridget said. "Not at all. Now we must do what we can to fix things before anyone else sees you like this."

"You have to stay out of sight, Jenny," I said.

"For just how long must I be cooped up here like a misbehaving chicken?" asked Jenny sulkily. "This is my vacation day. I wish to enjoy it."

"You can enjoy it after I bring you some proper clothes," Bridget replied, "though it's tempting to leave you locked up all day. That way I could enjoy the celebrations myself without worrying about you getting into trouble again."

"Not all day—" I began.

"Of course not, Ted," snapped Bridget. "That would be cruel. But Jenny mustn't be seen until she looks like herself again. We'll keep her safely here until I have her properly dressed."

"But, Cousin, I've already missed the opening celebrations—"

"I also missed them, Jenny, thanks to your foolishness," Bridget said. "So I'll hear no complaints from you. You almost caused a great deal of trouble today. The least you can do is be patient for a while until I have you respectably clothed again. Perhaps you could fill the time until I return by removing that ridiculous paint, or bootblack, or whatever it is, from your face."

"But, Bridget, I wanted to watch the races, and they've already begun! If I delay much longer, I shall nae see anything at all."

"And whose fault would that be?" Bridget asked. "I'll hurry, Jenny. The Hotel de France is only a few steps from here. I'll be back in no time at all with some of my clothes for you to wear."

"Thank you," a subdued Jenny said, but I scarcely heard her.

The races! I had almost forgotten. I had to withdraw our entry in the Three-Legged Race! I didn't want anyone else wondering who the mysterious Joseph Morrison was and why he hadn't shown up. As far as I was concerned, the fewer people who heard his name, the better. Joseph was about to vanish for good, and I didn't want anyone to ask about him. I had to tell the officials we wouldn't be racing, but...

"What shall I say?" I asked Bridget. "How can I explain why we won't be in the race?"

She laughed. "Just say your racing partner isn't himself today."

In spite of everything that had happened, I also laughed.

"No, 'he' most assuredly is not himself." We both turned and stared at Jenny, who lowered her head.

"I hope never to see Joseph again," Bridget said. "I've had enough of Master Morrison to last me the rest of my life."

"I agree," I said.

Jenny, for once, said nothing at all.

Eleven

I ran back to the main street, pushing through the crowd, trying to reach the officials at the starting line. "Excuse me, please, let me pass."

"Good luck, sir...Ted."

"Peter? What are you doing here?"

"I came to see you win the race. You and Joseph. Why are you so late?"

"I don't have time to explain," I said. "But we won't be in the race."

"Why? Where is Joseph?" Peter was now beside me, both of us trying to make our way politely through the street.

"I'll tell you later. Excuse me, ma'am. My apologies, sir."

"You will not get a refund of your entry fee," Peter said, following me.

"I know that."

We finally reached the starting line. The other contestants were ready, their legs bound. An official was calling my name. "Ted MacIntosh, come to the starting line with your partner at once. The Three-Legged Race is about to begin. Report immediately."

There were five other sets of competitors, but at the end of the lineup there was an empty space with two pieces of cloth in front of it.

Peter was right. I wouldn't get back the dollar entry fee. Even though I hadn't paid it, now that I knew who had, I hated to see it lost. But if I won the race, then I could give Jenny back her dollar and...

"Peter! You'll be my partner."

"Me?"

"Yes. If you will."

"I would enjoy that. Yes."

"But your name isn't Joseph. What if someone recognizes you?"

He stood still for a moment. "Joseph, Peter, Sing Kee, Kwok Leong—no one will recognize me, Ted. To most people one Chinese looks like every other one. Even those who know me as Peter will think I am Joseph if they are told that is my name."

"Really?"

"Yes. To white people we all look the same."

I didn't have time to think about that, though I found it difficult to believe. "Then today you'll be Joseph. He won't complain at all if you borrow his name. Believe me, *anyone* can be Joseph."

Peter looked puzzled, but he followed me and we took our place at the starting line. He bent to pick up the cloth ties and began to fasten our legs together. The official who had been calling my name nodded at me, then signalled to the starter. "All contestants are here," he said. "Let's begin."

Excitement built inside me. Peter and I were fast. We had

practised for many hours. We were very good. I knew we had an excellent chance to win. Jenny would be proud of me, of us. My parents would be proud, and I wouldn't have to share my half of the prize money with my father!

I snuck a quick glance at the other competitors. All of them were older. Two were giggling and could barely stand upright. These two had obviously been among those who had spent much of the night in a saloon. By their unsteady stance, I guessed they had continued drinking this morning. They wouldn't be difficult to beat.

I recognized another pair of racers. They both worked in Mason and Daly's General Store. They were clerks and weren't accustomed to physical exercise. Unless they had trained as hard as Peter and I, they wouldn't offer much competition, either.

There was no time to finish my assessment of the others. The starter lifted his pistol and said, "Take your marks."

Peter had finished binding our legs. He straightened, and we locked our arms around each other's waist. "We're going to win," I said. "I know it."

"I think so," Peter said, smiling. "We are good."

"Get ready," said the starter.

"Stop!" someone yelled.

"Get set," continued the starter.

"Stop," came the shout again, louder this time. "You must halt this race *immédiatement*."

The starter lowered his pistol. The official looked around, trying to see who was speaking. But I knew who it was. I recognized that voice. So I wasn't surprised when Henri Tremblay stepped forward.

"We do not allow animals to run with men," he said. "This race, it is only for men, *n'est-ce pas?* Not animals."

The starter seemed confused. "But there are no dogs here today. Not like last year."

"*Je ne parle pas de*—I do not speak of dogs," Henri Tremblay said. "But of that animal there." He gestured toward Peter.

"Animal?" the official said. "I don't see—"

"A heathen Chinese," Henri Tremblay said. "An evil animal."

The crowd gasped. I think many people hadn't realized until that very moment that my partner was Chinese. There had been a lot of activity at the starting line, and Peter had been bent over, fastening our legs. Now he stooped again and began to untie them. "No," I said, trying to pull him back to his feet. "You have as much right to be here as I do."

"In your eyes alone, sir...Ted," he said. "It is best if I go." He stayed crouched, his head bowed, though he had finished untying our legs.

"No, you must stay and race."

The people who had gathered to watch were becoming noisy. I could hear loud, angry voices. Although it seemed as if everyone was talking at once, I managed to hear fragments of sentences. "How dare he?" "Imagine, thinking he's as good as us!" "They're all liars and cheats, evil, scheming—just like one of those Chinamen to try to win money from honest white men."

I raised my voice to be heard over the commotion. "This is my friend. I invited him to race with me. Our entry fee is paid."

The starter and the race official were examining a piece of paper. I could see that it was the entry form where I had written my name. And Joseph Morrison's.

"I've changed my partner, that's all," I said. "There's no rule against that."

The starter looked at me, then at Peter. The official moved closer. He stared at me, and at Peter.

Henri Tremblay grinned at me, then spat on the ground in front of Peter. "So the boy brings one of his heathen friends to the races."

Spectators and racers had formed a circle around Peter and me. Peter was still crouched at my feet, his head bent as if he were trying to hide his face. "Stand up," I hissed at him, pulling on his arm. "Stand up. We've done nothing to be ashamed of."

Peter didn't answer me. He shook his head slightly and remained where he was.

The starter spoke and the throng fell silent. "This isn't Joseph Morrison," he said, pointing at Peter. "These Celestials have heathen names, and Joseph Morrison is a good Christian name."

"Peter will be my partner for the race," I said. "Joseph was...delayed."

"He can't be your partner," the official said. "Chinamen aren't allowed to compete in the races."

"That isn't fair," I said. "There's a Siwash Race for Indian men. Why can't a Chinese person also race?"

"The Indians race only against themselves," replied the starter. "They know their places and don't try to mix with their betters. No white man can enter the Siwash Race. No Indian or Chinaman can enter the other races."

"Where do the rules say that?" I asked.

"It isn't written down," the official said, "but everyone knows it. Isn't that so?" He turned and appealed to the crowd. "How say you all? Do we allow this Celestial to compete in the race?"

The mob roared, "No!"

The official nodded. "We agree then. But there's no reason why Ted shouldn't race. His entry fee is paid. Is there a man here who will be his partner?"

"I will," someone said.

"Me, too," someone else called.

"There," the starter said to me. "You have a choice of partners. Choose one quickly and let's begin."

"I will not race with anyone else," I said. Heat rose in my face, and I knew I was turning red. But this time I wasn't blushing. I was mad. "Peter is my friend. He lives in this country, in this town. He and his family work here. He has as much right to participate in the Dominion Day celebrations as any of us. He *will* run with me."

"No, he will not," the official said. "If you don't select another partner, then we'll begin the race without you. You've delayed us long enough."

"Step aside, boy," Henri Tremblay said, laughing. "*Oui*, step aside or you will be trampled by the feet of your betters."

"No!" I shouted. "I will not allow such an unfair thing to happen. These races are for everyone. All who pay their entry fee can enter them."

"Not true," a woman cried out. "Nae woman can race."

It was Jenny. Of course.

A few other women's voices joined in, agreeing with Jenny, and the noise grew louder. The starter raised his pistol and fired it. Silence fell immediately. The official sounded horrified when he spoke next. "No respectable woman would want to do such an unladylike thing as race in public. And no respectable man would run with a heathen. I fear there are many here who are disappointed in you, Ted MacIntosh."

"I *will* race with Peter," I said. "I demand you allow me to do so."

The starter turned to the race official and shook his head. Then the official spoke again, his voice impatient. "Ted MacIntosh, we have no quarrel with you, but you made an unwise decision when you asked this Celestial boy..."

He gestured to where Peter had been kneeling, but Peter was gone. My friend had slipped away so quietly that no one had noticed him leave. "See, your cowardly heathen partner has turned tail and fled," the official said. "Now you have no choice. Select another partner or withdraw from the race. This is the last time I shall ask."

"No!" I shouted. "I won't be part of such an unfair business. I'll stay right here until you allow me to race with the partner of my choice."

The starter laughed. "You don't have a partner now. If you will not move, I cannot make you. But be warned—you're likely to be trampled when the race begins." He gestured for the crowd to step back, lifted his pistol, and said, "Racers, take your marks."

The other runners returned to their positions at the starting line. I stayed where I was in front of them. Alone.

"I won't move!" I cried.

The starter lowered his pistol and gazed questioningly at the official. The official shrugged. "We'll proceed with the race, anyway," he said.

"I won't move," I said again. "I'll stay here and—"

"Be mowed down like a piece of wheat before the thresher, causing your poor mother much grief," my father said. "Stop this, son. It will do no good." He put a hand firmly on my shoulder, trying to push me away from the starting line. "I agree with you. It isn't fair, but there is nothing you can do about it."

"No, Pa, I won't move." I shook his hand off and faced the other runners.

They stared back. By the expressions on their faces, I could see they wouldn't alter their courses to avoid colliding with me. Several of them looked angry enough to run into me deliberately.

"Come with me, son," Pa said. "Please. Your mother is upset enough. Spare her any more embarrassment." I hadn't seen my mother in the crowd, but I knew she would be there, waiting hopefully to see me and Joseph win.

"No. I won't leave. I'll stay right here."

My father sighed. "Well, then I'll stay with you. We'll stand together, and be mowed down together, no doubt."

The starter lifted his pistol once more and said again, "Racers, take your marks."

"Quickly, Pa. Move out of the way."

My father shook his head. He had turned so he, too, faced the racers. Some of them lowered their eyes and wouldn't look at him.

"Get ready," called the starter.

I glanced at the other runners again. I had no doubt they would run right over us. I was strong and young and could withstand being pushed and shoved as they raced for the finish, but my father wasn't so young. I couldn't let him be harmed.

Taking a deep breath, I put my arm around my father, and the two of us walked toward the side of the road, away from the starting line. Behind us I heard the command "Get set..."

The crowd parted, letting us pass through. No one was watching the start of the race. All eyes were on us.

"I shall nae enjoy this race at all," said a woman wearing a hat with a dark veil. "I nae wish to observe any competitions that don't treat everyone as equals." She raised her voice. "Are there not others who feel as I do?" Although I didn't recognize either the dress or the hat she wore, I knew very well it was Jenny. She fell into step behind me and my father.

"Nor do I wish to watch," my mother said. "I've had enough of this sport. I'm also leaving."

"I don't like to hear any people called such names," another woman said. "It wasn't necessary to shame that young Chinese boy so." She turned her back on the racers and followed us.

"Although I wouldn't want to race in these rough competitions," yet another woman's voice said, "it wouldn't harm the men's pride if we women had our own race, something dignified such as the Egg and Spoon." She, too, began to walk away.

"Go!" said the starter, the word almost lost under the crack of his pistol. I heard the uneven thumping of feet as the race began, but only a few male voices were shouting encouragement to the competitors. It was strangely silent. I turned around to see what was happening.

Most of the women who had been in the crowd were behind Pa and me. Led by Jenny and my mother, they were ignoring the race. Many of the remaining spectators weren't watching the race, either. They were staring at us.

The procession remained close on our heels all the way down the main street until we could no longer hear the subdued cheering. Then, in a flurry of skirts, chatter, and raised sun parasols, the "parade" dispersed.

"Well..." Pa said. He sighed again, but this time I think it was due to relief.

"Well, indeed," said my mother.

The mysterious woman in the dark veil said nothing at all. She just lifted a small hand to wave goodbye.

"Don't forget tonight," I called to Jenny. "After the performance at the Theatre Royal is over, I'll meet you where I met Joseph and we'll watch the fireworks together. All three of us."

"Perhaps," she said without turning around, "though you didn't race with Joseph as you promised, so I do nae have to keep my promise."

"But I thought—"

"Well, maybe I'll be there. You'll have to wait and see what I decide."

Surely she would come, I thought. Surely she wouldn't hold me to that silly promise to race with "Joseph."

"I'll wait for you," I called to her retreating back. "Please come. Please."

"Perhaps," she said once more, then was gone.

"She'll be there," Pa said. "Don't fret, lad."

"Who?" Ma asked, looking from Pa back to me. "Who will be there?"

Pa grinned. I didn't answer. Ma glanced at Pa again, then back at me. Pa's grin grew broader. I said nothing, though I believe I blushed.

"Oh," Ma said. "Well, I understand. I think I understand." There was still a question on her face, but all she asked me was: "Shall we expect you home for dinner then? Or will you stay in town until evening?"

"Of course I'll come home to eat," I said. "But first there's something I have to do."

Twelve

I said goodbye to my parents and, only because my mother insisted, stopped briefly at the carpentry shop to change my clothes. "You're growing so fast you already strain the seams of your suit, Ted," she said. "In truth, I'm glad you didn't run in that race. You were wearing your good suit and would have destroyed what little wear is left in it."

Changing quickly, I headed to Chinatown, almost running along the deserted back street, avoiding the races that, by the shouts and cheers, were still in progress. I had to find Peter and apologize. That apology should come from many, including Henri Tremblay, the race officials, and the spectators who had called him names, but I knew I would be the only one to offer it.

I needed to apologize, for I was the one who had caused the problem. I had to tell Peter I was sorry for what had happened, even though I knew words were a poor salve for the pain caused by other words that sprang from hate.

Peter had disappeared before the others and I left the races. He didn't know that not everyone in Barkerville thought he was an "animal," that others had walked away in protest because of the way he had been treated. If I told him about that, it might help.

He had endured a great deal of humiliation because I had asked him to be my partner. What had I been thinking? Why hadn't I considered the consequences? Was I afraid of being labelled a coward if I withdrew my entry? Was I too greedy to give up a chance to win ten dollars? Too frugal to waste the entry fee, even though Jenny, not I, had paid it?

At that moment from farther down the street in the centre of Chinatown I heard laughter. Then a man's voice. "Run, dog! You wish to race? So run on the ground on your knees."

Again there was laughter. I picked up my pace, following the voices.

"Crawl. On the ground."

"That's where animals belong, Celestial. On the ground."

"Now we'll see you race. Ready, set, go!"

"Crawl, or you will regret it, heathen."

I found them in a small alleyway between two buildings. Three men were staring at something on the ground. I heard a thump, the noise of a boot hitting flesh, and a small yelp of pain.

Then I heard Peter, his voice loud and clear. "I will *not* crawl. I am not animal."

"You will do what we tell you to. *Immédiatement.* Crawl, I say. Now!"

"Stop!" I shouted. "Leave him alone."

The men turned around, and Henri Tremblay stepped away from the group. On the ground was Peter. He was kneeling, but his head was held high. Blood dripped from his forehead. He struggled to get to his feet when he saw me, but the man holding him wouldn't let him rise.

"Leave him alone," I repeated. "He's only a boy."

"So another boy comes to help him." Henri Tremblay moved toward me. "Come, boy who is almost *docteur*, play with your heathen friend on the ground like animals play. We will watch you race with him."

"Leave Peter alone," someone said. "Let him go at once." It was a strong, angry voice. I almost turned to see who had spoken, then realized it was me.

"So who will make us?" the Frenchman snarled.

"I will."

"You wish to fight, boy? *Bon.* Now you will learn that *enfants* must not be rude to their elders." There was a flash of silver, and a knife appeared in his hand.

I stepped forward, not thinking. Henri Tremblay's hand slashed out at me, and a strap of my overalls flopped loose, cut through. I scarcely noticed and kept moving toward him.

The Frenchman retreated slightly, surprised. Behind him his two friends stared at me. "Leave Peter alone," I said once more. "All of you."

"Henri," one of the men said, "we've had our fun. Let's go."

"*Non.* I wish to teach this boy a lesson."

I raised my hands, fists clenched. "Come and try. But fight like a man. Put the knife away."

The Frenchman scowled. "I do not need a knife for courage, not when I see only an *enfant timide* before me." There was a thunk, and suddenly his knife quivered at my feet, the handle only inches away, the blade buried in the ground.

I dragged my eyes away from the knife and took a deep breath. "I'm ready."

"No!" a voice from behind me shouted. "We will deal with this."

I whirled around. Sing Kee and several other Chinese men stood in the entrance to the alleyway. They all had knives in their hands.

Sing Kee ignored me. "Leave Chinatown, Mr. Tremblay. Go, and take your friends with you."

Henri Tremblay said nothing.

"Let's get out of here," one of the Frenchman's friends said. "Come on." The man was sweating and seemed nervous. "We don't want to fight the heathens now. There'll be another time." He bent, pulled the knife from the ground, and gave it to the Frenchman. "Another time, Henri."

The Frenchman wiped the knife on a leg of his trousers. "*Non.* Let us teach the heathens—all of them—a lesson they will not forget."

Henri Tremblay's other friend said firmly, "No, Henri, not this time. There are too many. You fight if you want, but I'm leaving."

"An excellent idea," Sing Kee said. "Go at once."

"I'm leaving, too," the man who was sweating said. "I don't want to fight."

Henri Tremblay's two cronies moved slowly toward the street. The Frenchman looked at Sing Kee, then at the knives in the hands of the Chinese men. Glaring at Peter and me, he spat on the ground in front of Peter, turned abruptly, and followed his friends.

All the knives had disappeared. Sing Kee and the other

Chinese men stood aside while the three white men edged cautiously past them and out of the alleyway. Suddenly my knees were weak, and I felt as if I were going to be ill. Sinking to the ground, I put my head in my hands and took a few deep breaths. When the sick feeling passed, I raised my head and found myself alone.

The Chinese men, Sing Kee, Henri Tremblay, and his friends—everyone had vanished. Had it really happened? I wondered. I touched the cut strap of my overalls flapping loosely against my chest, then ran my fingers across the deep gash in the earth where Mr. Tremblay's knife had been.

Yes, it had happened.

Slowly I stood, but my knees were stronger now. Peter— where was he? More than ever I needed to talk to him. Where had he gone? With Sing Kee? Yes, surely Sing Kee had taken Peter to his store to tend to the boy's injuries.

But when I pushed open the door of the herbalist's shop and called for Peter, there was no answer. "Peter, are you here?" I called again.

Sing Kee emerged from behind the curtain that screened the back room. "Go away, Master Theodore," he said, frowning. "You have caused much trouble today."

"I need to see Peter. Is he here?"

"You must look for Peter elsewhere. Go home."

"But I have to make sure he's all right. He was bleeding."

"I have cleaned the cut and applied a salve. It is not serious." He turned his back and went to his workbench.

"I need to see him," I repeated.

"No, you do not. His own people will care for him, Master Theodore. Now please leave."

Sing Kee always called me Ted, not the formal Master Theodore. He was very angry with me.

"I'm sorry, Sing Kee. I didn't mean to cause trouble for Peter. Please understand that."

"Sorry is only a word. It will not help right now. My nephew is hurt, both in body and spirit. Leave him alone. Let him heal." The herbalist leaned over his large stone mortar and began grinding dried herbs into a fine powder, the heavy pestle thumping noisily against the curved sides of the mortar.

"Sing Kee, please..."

The sound of pounding grew louder. Sing Kee concentrated on his work, as if I weren't there. He didn't answer me, and I knew there was no use trying to talk to him. Once more I said, "I'm truly sorry," then left.

Perhaps Peter would be with his father, but Mr. Lee met me at the door of his store. "Peter not here," he said before I could say anything. "Go away." He, too, was upset, and I didn't stay to question him further. "I'm sorry for the trouble, Mr. Lee. Please forgive me. Please tell Mrs. Lee I'm very, very sorry."

"Go away," Peter's father again said. "You go now." I went.

Maybe Peter was at the restaurant where he used to work. Nervously I made my way there. Although Henri Tremblay and his friends had been in a hurry to leave Chinatown the last time I saw them, this was a place where they often ate. To my relief neither the Frenchman nor any of his friends was in the restaurant. Neither was any other white person. The owner ran to me the moment I stepped in the door, shaking his head and waving his hands as though to push me away. "Closed, we closed, go." The restaurant was completely silent. Everyone stared at me, and I saw anger on their faces.

"I'm truly sorry for what happened," I said.

Not a single voice replied. No one here would help me find Peter, I realized, so I turned and left.

There was nowhere else for me to search except at Peter's own home. But I didn't know where he lived, and even if I could find his house, the thought of facing his mother made me ill. If strangers in the restaurant, and Sing Kee, my friend, were angry, how would Peter's mother feel toward me? How could I apologize to her for being the cause of her son's humiliation—and his injury? Someday Peter might forgive me, but I doubted that his mother ever would.

I retraced my steps to Sing Kee's. He *must* know where Peter was. He was his uncle. I would try one last time to get him to tell me.

Sing Kee was at his workbench. He looked up in surprise when I came in. Then he frowned. "What do you want?"

"Sing Kee, you must know where Peter is. Please tell me."

"I thought you had gone home."

"No. I've been looking for him."

"All this time?"

"Yes. I have to speak to him, Sing Kee. He was hurt because of me. I need to tell him I'm sorry."

Sing Kee shook his head. "I told you that it was not a serious injury."

"I need to see for myself. Do you know where he is?"

Sing Kee sighed. "I have said that you must look for Peter elsewhere."

Something about the way he answered didn't sound right. "You *do* know where he is, don't you?"

"You must look for—"

"You're not answering my question. Please help me find him."

"If you cannot find him, then perhaps he does not want to be found." Sing Kee picked up a jar of herbs, uncorked it, and dropped a handful into a small pot. He avoided my eyes.

I was silent for a while. "Yes," I said at last, "I understand. At least I think I do."

Sing Kee said nothing.

"I understand," I said again. "Peter doesn't want to see me."

Sing Kee remained silent.

Tears stung my eyes, and I forced them back. "Peter has every right to be angry. But please, Sing Kee, when you see him, tell him I apologize. Tell him I'm sincerely sorry for the embarrassment I caused him today. I'm sorry he was made to..."

Once again I saw Peter on his knees surrounded by Henri Tremblay's jeering gang. Once more I saw the blood on his forehead. It was my fault. Everything that had happened to Peter today was because of me.

"Sing Kee, please, you must tell Peter I'm sorry. I had hoped he would forgive me—maybe someday he will—but I understand that he doesn't want to see me." I bowed respectfully to the herbalist and turned to leave.

I realized I would never see Peter again except perhaps on the street as we passed each other. I knew he would avoid me whenever he could, that we would no longer be friends. Once more tears rose behind my eyelids.

Peter could never forgive me for what had happened today. I wondered if I could ever forgive myself.

I was almost at the door when a voice called, "Do not go."

The curtain to the back room swung aside, and Peter walked through it. He had been crying and his voice was shaky. But the blood had been cleaned from his face and, to my relief, I could see he had only a small cut on his forehead.

"Peter, are you all right?"

"Yes. Most of me is."

"It was my fault, Peter. I'm so sorry."

"It is not your fault, sir...Ted. I wanted to race. I wanted to win."

"Please forgive me."

"There is nothing to forgive. My uncle says I was foolish. He uses many wise proverbs to explain. It was my mistake, not yours."

"You know what you did was wrong," Sing Kee said. "Our people do not need more trouble."

"Peter didn't plan to race with me," I said. "I asked him to be my partner at the last minute. It was my misjudgement, not Peter's."

Sing Kee frowned. "Perhaps, but Peter understands more than you do, Ted, how things are with the Chinese in this country. He knows better."

"Yes, Uncle," Peter said. There was silence for a while, then he smiled wanly. "But we run like wind together, Ted. We would have won."

"We would have won easily," I said, smiling back. "Perhaps next year..."

Sing Kee shook his head. "No. You must not think of it. You must stay in your place, Nephew, like other Chinese. Otherwise you cause much anger—and harm. Just one person, you, was hurt today, but more could have been injured."

"There were people who thought Peter was treated badly, Sing Kee. Jenny, my mother, and a great many other women left the races, saying it was unfair."

"Really?" Peter said.

"That is good," said Sing Kee. "But most men did not think it unfair, and it is the men, not the women, who make the laws. It is also the men who fight when they are angry."

Peter studied his feet. "Today I caused much trouble. I am sorry, Uncle."

"Yes," Sing Kee said. "Even Ted was angry. Mr. Tremblay seemed surprised that Ted would fight as fiercely as a tiger."

"Tiger? Oh, no, Sing Kee, I felt like a kitten."

"A very cross kitten, sir...Ted. A very brave kitten."

"Yes, brave enough to scratch hard," said Sing Kee, smiling for the first time.

"Mr. Tremblay and his friends are cruel men," Peter said, touching the cut on his forehead. "It is hard to believe that some men are so cruel, but others, like you and your father, are always kind and do not treat people differently."

"It is the same in China, Nephew," Sing Kee said.

"How can that be?" I asked. "In China you're all Chinese. How can you be treated differently there?"

"In China not all of us are equal," Sing Kee said. "Merchants like my brother are not held in high regard, for they must associate with foreign devils—excuse me, Ted—in their work."

I didn't much like being thought of as a foreign devil, but I supposed it wasn't much worse than being called a heathen animal, so I just nodded.

"Even field labourers more important than merchants like my father," Peter said. "For they help to create life."

"Here, in this new country, we hope to change the way

people think," Sing Kee said.

"Yes," Peter added, "we hope. But Mr. Tremblay and others like him..." He didn't finish the sentence, but shook his head and changed the subject. "You did not explain, Ted. Why did Mr. Joseph not come to race?"

I grimaced. "That isn't easy to explain." But I did.

Sing Kee covered a broad grin with his hand, and Peter laughed. "That Miss Jenny, she very unusual woman," Peter said.

"She is indeed," I agreed. "But please don't say anything about this prank of hers. Bridget is right. It wouldn't be considered a ladylike thing to do."

"We will not speak of it again," Sing Kee said, still grinning. "A wise man knows when to remain silent."

"When Miss Jenny is around, most people are silent," Peter said. "For she talks a great deal."

"Yes," I admitted, "but she has a beautiful voice, doesn't she?"

Thirteen

After I left Sing Kee's shop, thunder shook the sky and a few fat raindrops began to fall. Although the morning had dawned clear and bright, a storm was moving in. At any moment I knew the clouds would open and one of summer's heavy rainfalls would drench the town.

There were no more shouts or cheers—the contests were over. Even the horse racing must have finished, for the area around the platform was deserted when I passed. The rain would cause no problems now that most of the day's activities were completed. In fact, it would be welcome to those of us who hoped to watch the fireworks. There had been much discussion about the safety of the planned fireworks display, and some people thought it shouldn't be risked, not even to celebrate Dominion Day. One great fire had been enough, they said. It would be a tragedy to risk a second, merely for the pleasure of seeing a few coloured lights in the sky. But now that it was raining—if the rain wasn't too heavy by evening—the fireworks could safely be ignited. And Jenny and I would view them together. She had promised, hadn't she?

When I returned to town after dinner, the storm was over.

The streets were only slightly muddy and the air was cool. The mosquitoes and black flies had enjoyed the rain, and they were unusually fierce, but tonight I scarcely noticed them.

As I got closer to Pa's shop, I began to worry again. Would Jenny be there? Was she angry at me for not insisting she be allowed to race? But how could I have done that? Bridget had forbidden it. Surely Jenny would meet me. It wasn't my fault that "Joseph" and I couldn't race.

Then, from a distance, I spotted her on the boardwalk in front of Pa's shop. I walked faster. "Jenny!" I called, relieved. "You're here!"

"Yes," she said. "So I am."

I smiled. "I'm glad. It'll be a fine evening."

Jenny nodded, the black veil over her face fluttering as she did.

"That's a good idea, that hat with the veil," I said. "The insects are hungry tonight."

"Oh?" she said. "Aye, of course, the wee beasties. This veil does keep them from my face."

I slapped at a mosquito. "Come, let's go through the town and take in the displays. Most shops have been decorated to honour Dominion Day, and I didn't have time to see everything earlier."

"Nor did I," Jenny said, sighing. "I had nae planned on spending today in the house with the twins."

"I thought you had the whole day off. Didn't you tell me Mrs. Fraser said you could attend all the festivities?"

"Aye, but I changed my mind and stayed away from the celebrations."

"I didn't watch any races, either. I lost my enthusiasm for

them after Peter was treated so badly."

I didn't tell her how badly Henri Tremblay and his gang had treated Peter, that his humiliation hadn't ended at the starting line. No doubt she would find out what had happened, but until then I didn't want to speak about it to anyone.

"Eejit races. Eejit rules. Poor Peter." Jenny took my arm, and we stepped down from the boardwalk and began to stroll through the town, looking at the decorations. The performance at the Theatre Royal had ended, and other people were doing the same thing. Even though it wasn't fully dark yet, many stores had candles and lamps in their windows, illuminating Dominion Day displays.

In the window of Moses's barbershop was an evergreen wreath adorned with tiny ribbon rosettes surrounding a gold crown honouring Her Majesty, Queen Victoria. Many other windows also had crowns, though some had flags, wreaths, and garlands, as well. The Engine House and the adjoining Theatre Royal were trimmed with hooks, ladders, hoses, axes, and other implements of the Fire Brigade, all wreathed in evergreens. The German bakery displayed the colours of the new German empire, and the Union Jack flew from about twenty poles up and down the street.

Over the road hung banners proclaiming GOD SAVE THE QUEEN, UNION FOREVER, and SUCCESS TO THE DOMINION. More evergreens and ribbons in red, white, and blue, the colours of the Union Jack, festooned every available window and doorframe and were looped around the overhead water pipes.

"Oh," said Jenny, "the town looks almost bonny, not at all like its usual dreich self."

I didn't think Barkerville was "drab" at all, but I didn't want to disagree with Jenny. Not tonight.

We said hello to others along the way, though I was surprised how few people greeted us in return. Perhaps they didn't recognize Jenny in her black veil. But I had no time to worry about that because suddenly there was a series of explosions, and the sky lit up—the fireworks had begun!

We hurried to Chinatown. The street was packed; everyone had gathered where the fireworks were being assembled and lit.

Four shooting stars sped upward, exploding in a shower of tiny red lights. The crowd gasped, then clapped. There was another bang, and a large fireball flew high above our heads, bursting into hundreds of soft white stars that fell slowly to earth. The crowd roared with pleasure and surged forward.

I was roughly pushed aside as two laughing men made their way to the front of the crowd. "Watch where you're going, sirs," I said.

"Sorry!" they shouted without glancing back.

"Ow!" Jenny said, moving closer to me as she dodged another spectator who had shoved his way past us, intent on having the best possible view.

"Are you hurt?"

"Nae, not to cry about. Although someone just stood hard on my toe."

There was another spray of colour, another cheer from the crowd, another swell of movement around us. Once more I was bumped into. This time I nearly lost my footing, and Jenny gripped my arm tighter.

"Are *you* hurt?" she asked.

"No. I don't know why people have to push and shove to get a better view when all they have to do is glance up. Why, I'm sure the fireworks can be seen from anywhere in town."

"So they can. Let's leave."

"Where shall we go?"

"Someplace where there are nae so many rude people," she said, pulling on my arm and leading me back the way we had come. "I imagine the boardwalk outside your father's shop has an excellent view."

I laughed. "Perhaps 'Joseph' is still there waiting for us."

Jenny pulled her arm from mine. "Ted MacIntosh, I don't want to hear that name again. Kindly keep your feeble jokes to yourself. I would rather return to the Frasers and make sure the twins are properly tucked in for the night than stay here and listen to you blethering on about Joseph!"

"I'm sorry. Please don't be upset." I had seen both Bridget and Jenny angry once today. It was an experience I didn't want to repeat. "I promise I'll never mention him again."

"See that you don't. For I'm truly tired of the fellow." She replaced her arm in mine. The sky blazed again, this time with orange lights.

The boardwalk in this part of town was deserted. "You're right, Jenny," I said. "Most of the fireworks are exploding high above the rooftops. We have a good view from here."

"And nae one steps on my toes here, either," Jenny said, plopping onto the boardwalk stairs and pulling off one of her boots.

I averted my eyes while she rubbed her toes, then replaced the boot. "That's better," she said, then gasped. "Oh, the sky is all yellow!"

We could still hear the crowd cheering and clapping, but there was no one else around us. It was as if we had our own private display.

"See," I said, pointing, "three colours at once, and higher than the rest." I sat down beside Jenny.

"It's beautiful."

"Yes...beautiful." But I didn't mean the fireworks.

Jenny turned to me. She took one of my hands in hers and stared earnestly into my face. Or at least I think she was looking at my face. She still wore her hat with the black veil. "I must ask you a question, Ted."

"What? I'll tell you anything you want to know." I put my other hand on top of hers.

"I can nae forget about today and the Three-Legged Race until I know something. Will you answer me honestly?"

"As honestly as I can. What's the question?"

"Bridget said you would nae have been part of such a silly prank, that you thought it a glaikit—nae, a right eejit idea— and you were a sensible young man and wouldn't have raced with me at all, even if she hadn't stopped me."

I strongly suspected what Jenny's question would be. I also knew I didn't want to answer it. That I didn't *dare* answer it.

"Well? Would you have raced with me? Even though you knew it was me and not Joseph? Would you have done it?"

There was no way I could answer that question without angering her, so I said nothing. Instead I gently lifted the veil from her face, cupped my hands around her cheeks, and kissed her.

The sky brightened with the most brilliant of the fireworks yet, turning night into day for a few seconds. That was all the time it took to see, faint but unmistakable, the outlines of a large bootblack moustache still on Jenny's upper lip. I reached out a finger, touched it gently, then laughed.

"I scrubbed and scrubbed, but it would nae come off," Jenny said.

"Now I understand the mysterious veil."

She was close to tears. "It makes my face so ugly. I hope it will wear off soon."

"It doesn't matter," I said, and kissed her again, moustache and all.

The clouds had been gathering, and rain started once more just as the fireworks finished. Jenny and I made our way toward the Frasers' house, moving slowly even though we were both getting wet. Her arm tucked securely under mine, she leaned close as we walked. Rain or no rain, I didn't want the evening to end.

But the weather had other ideas. The rain increased, pouring out of the sky as if the clouds were emptying themselves of cauldrons of water all at once. We were forced to quicken our steps, running the last few yards. At the Frasers' porch Jenny took off her hat and shook the rain from it. Even though the only light came from a lamp in the front window, I could still see the faint outline of the moustache. She put her hand over it self-consciously. I laughed and gently pushed her hand away. "It's a memento of today," I said. "Of Jo— Of you know who."

"It's been a grand day, or at least the last part of it has. Although I'll carry the memory of it in my heart—" she smiled at me, and I knew I blushed "—I nae wished to carry a reminder like this on my face!"

"It will come off. Try rubbing it with lard mixed with fine sand. That mixture removes paint stains from my hands."

"So you wish me to be scratched raw and greasy-faced as well as moustache-faced, do you?"

"No, just be Jenny-faced once more."

"I'll scrub it again tonight, but with some of Mrs. Fraser's cold cream, not with lard and sand. I can nae go out in public in the daylight until this thing is gone."

"Wear your veil as you did today and no one will notice."

"Perhaps. Although this hat is nae suitable for summer wear. People will wonder why I chose it instead of a bonnet."

Silence fell. "Jenny..." I began, then sneezed.

"You have a long walk home. It's time for you to go."

"But—" I said, then sneezed again.

"Be off with you, Ted MacIntosh. Quickly now. You're wet enough already. You'll take a cold if you're not careful."

"I'm not very wet," I protested.

Jenny shook her head and reached for the door latch. "You're drenched. Now go home. Perhaps I'll see you tomorrow?"

"As soon as I can get away from work," I promised, sneezing again. "Good night, Jenny."

"Good night, Ted. It's been a most enjoyable—nae, a most wonderful—evening."

"Yes," I said. "Yes, it has been."

She pushed open the door and went inside. I stood alone on the porch for a moment, then stepped off into the rain and headed home.

For the first time in years the Richfield road didn't frighten me and I wasn't nervous to be on it in the dark. I didn't walk faster as I usually did when I travelled here alone, sometimes almost running in my eagerness to reach the comfort and safety of home. Tonight I didn't look behind or ahead of me, fearful of what, or whom, I might see.

Tonight I was scarcely aware I was moving. It seemed as if my feet weren't touching the ground, as if my boots were as light as dancing slippers, not heavy with mud, as if my feet glided inches above the ground. My head was too full of other things to make room for ghosts or murderers or any of the terrors, real and imagined, that had so often followed me along this road. My heart was too light to dwell on dark happenings from the past.

The rain beat on my back, but I barely felt it. It dripped steadily through the trees, splashing noisily into the wagon ruts, but I hardly heard it. There was music all around me, and when I stopped and listened, wondering who was singing, I was amazed that it was me.

Fourteen

When I awoke the next morning, the singing had stopped. So had the rain. Through the open curtains of my bedroom window I saw sunlight. It must be very hot outside, I thought. I was sweating; my sheets were damp and clammy.

I dressed slowly, and though I wasn't very hungry, I went for breakfast.

"Did you enjoy the fireworks?" my father asked.

"Very much," I said, sneezing.

"You're sick!" my mother said.

"No," I insisted, but then became aware of an uncomfortable feeling in my throat. "At least I don't think I am."

"You look unwell," Ma said. "All that fuss yesterday was too much for you. You've taken a cold. Let me feel your forehead. You're feverish!"

"I'm fine, Ma."

"You don't look fine. You're pale and there are big circles beneath your eyes. *I* was never a doctor's apprentice, but I know when my son is ill."

Pa studied me. "He does look peaked. We don't have much

work today. Stay home, son."

"An excellent idea," Ma said. "After that disgraceful business yesterday, a day's rest will be good for him."

What did my mother mean by "disgraceful business"? Had Jenny and I been seen? "Ah...I can explain..." I spluttered.

"Look at the lad," my father said to my mother. "He must be really ill. His face is flaming red." They both stared hard at me.

"About yesterday, Ma, it was—"

"A most distressing day." My mother shook her head. "Yes, that poor child. Peter was treated so dreadfully by the officials at the races."

"The race! You mean what happened at the race, not—"

"I meant the race, though by the way you're blushing there's more you haven't told me. For instance, how you managed to cut the strap of your overalls. You could begin your explaining there."

"Nae, don't press the lad," my father said firmly. "He was a credit to us yesterday the way he defended Peter."

My mother's face softened. "It took courage to stand by your friend. I was proud of you, though it was most dismaying for me to watch. I feared that the other racers would run you and your father down. It's a wonder you weren't hurt."

"It is indeed," my father said.

From the look he gave me I knew he wasn't just speaking about the race. Although I had told my parents nothing about my encounter with Henri Tremblay and his friends in Chinatown, I realized my father had heard what had happened. "I'm sorry about my overalls," I said.

"Your mother can mend them for you, son. If not, a pair

of overalls is a small price to pay. The cost could have been much greater."

"I'm sorry," I said, "but I couldn't—"

"We'll talk later," Pa said. "Now is not the time to discuss it." He glanced at my mother. "I'll go to work and leave your mother to doctor you to her heart's content. I think you've earned a day of rest."

"Thank you, Pa."

"But when you're rested, we'll speak," he continued. "There's only a thin line between bravery and stupidity. If you insist on being dangerously brave, there are some manly arts you need to learn so you can defend yourself."

"What are you talking about?" Ma asked.

"Nothing," Pa and I answered together.

"I'll discuss this 'nothing' with you later, Ian," my mother said sternly to my father. "When a man says 'nothing,' he usually means there's a great deal of 'something' going on."

Neither my father nor I replied. Pa quickly finished his breakfast, kissed Ma, patted me on the shoulder, and left.

I stirred my spoon in the bowl of porridge. Manly arts? Did Pa wish me to learn to box? Although I had raised my fists and challenged Henri Tremblay yesterday, I knew nothing of fighting and had no desire to learn. Or did he want me to learn how to use a knife? I didn't want to do that, either.

I would talk to Jenny about Pa's plans, once he told me what they were. Jenny would know what I should do.

Jenny! I had promised to meet her today. I wanted to see her. I needed to see her. I couldn't stay home.

"Your face is very red again, Ted." My mother was bearing down on me with a spoon and a green glass bottle.

"I feel..." I began, but was interrupted by a bout of coughing.

When I regained my breath, my mother had filled the spoon and was holding it in front of me. "Take some of this. It works well on colds and fevers. You prepared it yourself for me when I was ill while you were apprenticed to Dr. Wilkinson."

Obediently I opened my mouth and allowed her to dose me with a large spoonful of the thick syrup. I grimaced as I swallowed, wishing I had used more sugar when I blended that particular batch of medicine. "I feel much better," I said. "I think I'll go to work, after all."

My mother looked hard at me, and I stayed put.

In truth, much as I wanted to see Jenny I was glad to be at home. My cough grew worse during the day, my face burned hot and red, and the tickle in my throat became a searing pain. I remained in bed, allowed my mother to bring me tea and soup, and meekly swallowed more medicine without complaining.

The day passed, though I didn't remember much of it. I coughed, dozed, then slept more. I didn't realize it was evening until Pa returned from work and woke me, shaking me gently.

"Ted? Son, how are you?"

"I don't know," I said, struggling to push myself upright. "My throat hurts and my head feels peculiar."

"You've done naught but sleep all day, your mother tells me."

"Have I? Is the day over?"

"It is, and it's been full of news."

"What news?"

"Judge Crease has arrived. The Assizes begin tomorrow."

"The trial—at last."

"Yes. Mr. Mow will have justice after all these months."

"The trial is tomorrow? I must go to it." Then I lay back down. My head was too heavy to hold up anymore. "I was there at the beginning," I said, thinking again of the smell of blood steaming in the cold November air. "I want to be there at the end."

"You haven't been called as a witness, but I agree you must attend the trial, even though you're ill." Pa's face was serious. "I've heard it said that you're afraid of Tremblay, which is why you didn't come to work today. They're saying you're cowering at home, too frightened to face the Frenchman."

"I'm not afraid of him or his friends," I said, struggling to sit up again. "Who says that?"

"Those who don't believe you were so badly injured in the fight that you're near death and can't stir from your bed."

"I wasn't injured, and I'm not afraid! I've taken a cold, that's all. You know that, Pa."

"Aye, but you must be seen in public so that others may know it, too."

"I will be at the trial," I said with determination.

"So shall I," my father said.

"You don't need to go, Pa. There's work to be done in the shop."

"The work can wait," he said, then was silent for a moment. "Although you haven't told me everything that happened between you and Tremblay, I've heard much about it. If even half of it's true, you were brave but also foolhardy."

I said nothing. I hadn't thought about being brave, just about Peter being hurt and kneeling on the ground with his head held high.

"I'm proud of your courage," Pa said, "but I'll come to the trial with you. When a man faces enemies, it's a comfort to have his father by his side."

"What man?" I asked, bewildered.

"You, son."

"Me?"

"Aye."

"I told you, I'm not afraid of Mr. Tremblay."

"Perhaps not. But though you don't realize it yet, he isn't your only enemy. Not any longer."

"Enemies? How have I made enemies? I've angered no one except Mr. Tremblay and his friends."

"That may be what you believe, but there are others who feel you shouldn't have championed a Chinese boy, that you lowered yourself when you befriended a Celestial. Many people have come by the shop today and told me I should teach my son his proper place so he doesn't repeat such shameful actions in the future. The chief constable even suggested a trip to the woodshed."

"A licking?" I was horrified. "He suggested a licking?"

Pa grinned. "I suppose I should consider it, Ted, for you've been up to a great deal of mischief lately. But you know I've never raised a hand against you, and I wouldn't do so now. However, your actions have been taken more seriously than you realize. Some townsfolk have told me that if I wish to keep their business I must prevent you from making a fool of yourself as you did yesterday."

I sat up straighter, my weakness forgotten. "Who says I've been making a fool of myself?"

Pa sighed. "It doesn't matter. But there's been much talk, some very ugly, not just about the Three-Legged Race but also about your fight with the Frenchman and his cronies."

"They were hurting Peter! What else could I have done?"

"You did what your heart told you to do, son. You always will."

"Many white men play cards and gamble with Chinese men. How is it different if I run a race with a Chinese boy? Racing, playing cards—both are only games!"

"Others see it differently, son."

"That's not fair."

"I agree. It isn't fair. I think the gambling is part of the reason the Chinese are so disliked. They're canny card players and often win. Sometimes a great deal of money changes hands, and those who lose it become enraged against all Chinese."

"But that has nothing to do with Peter racing with me."

Pa rubbed a hand over his face. I heard the scratch of his callused palm against new whisker growth. "You and I see no difference between a card game and a race, Ted. But others do. I'll be with you at the trial to show all who are there that I believe you've done no wrong."

"I *haven't* done anything wrong."

"Some people perceive it as wrong."

"Then some people are stupid."

My father laughed. "I agree. But we can't change the nature of this town, nor of the people in it. They'll talk and they'll have opinions. When that talk and those opinions are against my son, I don't like it, but I can do little about it except stand by his side." He stood, his knees creaking as he did. "Last night's damp makes my bones ache. Now I'll go and explain all, or as much as I dare, about your fight with Tremblay to your mother. That conversation, I've no doubt, will make my head ache, as well."

"Does she have to know?" I asked.

"Aye. She's bound to find out when she next goes to town. Your name is on everyone's lips, and some nosy glib gabbit will delight in telling her what you've been up to. It might be wise if you bided your time here for a while, safe in bed and out of your mother's way."

I had no wish to get up, so I nodded and lay down again when Pa left the room. My head whirled. I thought of the ugly comments I had heard around me at the starting line, of the names Peter had been called, of the blood on his face. Was I wrong to be angered by that? How could anyone not be?

My parents were talking in the kitchen. Their voices were low, and only once could I make out their words.

"He's so young, Ian," my mother said.

"Not so young, not anymore. You can't keep him a babe safe in your arms all his life."

I think Ma began to cry, but I heard no more. Closing my eyes, I let sleep take me.

The next morning I awoke, feeling clearheaded and rested, but my throat was still quite sore. Perhaps I had learned more than I had thought when I worked with Dr. Wilkinson, for though I could no longer remember the ingredients of the syrup I had prepared, whatever was in it had eased my cough.

My father had already left so that he could put in a morning's work before going to the courthouse. But there was no need for me to go until later. The trial wouldn't begin until noon.

Ma insisted I eat a substantial breakfast, and I did so, though it hurt when I swallowed. She didn't speak much, but kept peering at me anxiously. I had the feeling that after Pa talked to her the previous night there was a great deal she wished to say to me. But it appeared she had decided to keep the words to herself for now.

"I'm much better, Ma," I reassured her.

"This morning it isn't how *you* feel that worries me, Ted. It's how others feel *about* you."

I bent my head over my porridge and ate silently. There was nothing I could say.

"I've ironed your suit. You must look your best at the trial."

"Thank you, Ma."

She hugged me. "Eat. Finish your breakfast. You need strength today." She turned away quickly, but not before I saw tears in her eyes. She wouldn't allow me to leave the house until I took more cough syrup.

"Please, Ma, don't fret about me."

"It is a mother's job to fret about her children, Ted. I wish you didn't have to go. I wish you—"

"I feel much better," I told her again, though I knew that wasn't what she had meant.

The last of the rain clouds had emptied from the sky, and now swarms of insects buzzed happily in the warm air. There were fresh prints across the road near our house—deer and porcupine—and I could see where the animals had stopped to drink the rainwater that had pooled in the wagon ruts. Steam rose gently from puddles, and in the woods birds sang cheerfully.

I didn't sing, nor was I cheerful. Although I didn't feel as ill as I had the day before, I was glad the trial would be at the courthouse in Richfield. It was a shorter journey from my home to Richfield than it was the other way to Barkerville. But in this direction the road wound uphill and was steep. By the time I reached the courthouse, I was sweating and out of breath. I paused and leaned against a large tree, breathing deeply, trying to stifle a fit of coughing. Pulling a handkerchief from my pocket, I swabbed my face, wishing I hadn't worn my wool suit. The heat had increased, and I wondered if my fever had also returned. My legs felt weak, my throat burned, and my head ached.

But it didn't matter how I felt. I had to be at this trial.

There were many people gathered in front of the large white courthouse, determined to be first in line when the doors were opened. I heard voices and laughter. In the gold fields legal proceedings sometimes offered as much entertainment as theatre productions. It had seemed as if the whole town had come to watch Ah Mow's inquest.

But the inquest had been held at the Theatre Royal, not here. Once I had watched another trial in this courthouse. Then, too, there were many spectators, all anxious to learn the fate of a man accused of murder. When the trial was over, gallows were erected in front of the courthouse and a man had been hanged.

I pushed away from the tree, no longer grateful for its support. It had been here, sitting behind this very tree, on this exact spot, that I had heard the sounds of that execution. I had been forbidden to watch, but I had disobeyed my parents and gone. I hadn't seen what had happened, only listened. Even so, the sounds I had heard that evening had found their way into my nightmares for many years.

Suddenly words came from behind me. "Sir...Ted."

I jumped. "Peter! I'm glad to see you. Are you going to the trial, too?"

"No, we must wait out here."

Although I hadn't noticed them before, a large group of Chinese men were assembled under the shade of a cotton-wood tree near the courthouse. "Peter, your head!" He was no longer bleeding, but his forehead was covered by a dark bruise from the centre of which rose a large lump. "Does it hurt?"

Peter touched the bruise. "No, it does not hurt. But if you had not come to help me..."

"I'm sorry for—"

"Do not be sorry. I learned much on Dominion Day. And I took only small harm for all that learning. You will go inside and listen to what is said in the court?"

"Yes."

"Will you tell the judge what you saw?"

"I haven't been asked to be a witness, Peter. I can't say anything, not unless the judge asks me to."

He fingered the bruise on his forehead again. "I wish you could speak to the jury, sir...Ted."

"If I'm asked, I'll speak. I promise. Ah Mow will find justice, Peter. Trust me. The jury will listen to all the evidence. The men who saw the murder will testify, and Henri Tremblay will be punished."

"I hope so. But it would be good if you could speak in the court for Ah Mow. Speak for all of us Chinese people."

"Ted, it's time." My father had arrived.

"Yes, Pa."

"I will wait here," Peter said. "I hope it will not be a long trial."

"Me, too," I said. My throat was so sore I could barely speak. I wished I had a drink of water to soothe it.

"We'll tell you everything that happens, Peter," my father promised. "But now we have to go if we're to find a seat."

"Don't worry, Peter," I said. "Everything will be all right."

My father and I joined the queue in front of the courthouse. The doors swung open. "Court will begin in ten minutes," Chief Constable Lindsay announced from the front steps. "Please enter, but remember to conduct yourselves with respect." The crowd surged forward, eager for the best seats. Pa and I followed.

"Welcome, gentlemen," the chief constable said. "I've saved you two excellent seats. The jury, all fine men of the gold fields, has been selected, and the judge is well fed and eager to begin. I'm sure this proceeding won't take long. Come in, come in."

I had my mouth open to thank him when two men behind us pushed forward. Chief Constable Lindsay greeted them warmly and ushered them to seats near the front. I felt myself turning red as I realized he hadn't been speaking to Pa and me, that he had deliberately ignored us.

"Pa—"

"Let it be, son. Pay the constable and his rudeness no mind."

I was upset, though I tried to hide it. The chief constable had always been friendly toward me...until now.

Pa and I found seats near the back, the second to last row. Already the courthouse was nearly full, though I could hear other would-be spectators arriving outside. Sing Kee sat in the front row. I knew he would be the translator for some of the witnesses. In the prisoner's box, seated on a small bench behind wooden railings, was Henri Tremblay.

Once again I would be present at a man's trial. Once again I would listen as witnesses testified, lawyers argued, and the jury delivered a verdict. Would I also once again see a judge place a black cloth over his head and sentence a man to death?

Would there be another hanging in the gold fields?

Fifteen

The door leading to the judge's chambers opened, and Judge Crease entered the courtroom. He strode to the bench without looking around him, his head high, steps firm.

"All rise," the court clerk called.

The judge took his place, and once we were all seated again, nodded at us and began his opening remarks. "This court is now convened. I remind you that I am the Queen's representative, and any disrespect shown to me, or my position, is disrespect shown to Her Majesty, Queen Victoria. There have been occasions during other court sessions in the gold fields where the spectators have shown no respect for the solemnity of the proceedings. There has even been shouting and unruly laughter in this courthouse. These disgraceful exhibitions of disrespect will *not* be tolerated. Only those citizens summoned as witnesses, the foreman of the jury, or the learned counsel presenting the case may speak here. And I remind them all to address me as My Lord. I will tolerate no inappropriate or disrespectful behaviour in my courtroom. Is that perfectly clear to everyone?"

There was complete silence. The judge scowled, then

leaned back in his seat, satisfied he had been understood. "Very well. Then let us proceed with as much haste as possible. There is a full, unusually heavy calendar for these Assizes. One indictment for the most serious offence in the eyes of God or man—murder. Three for stabbing, and one for breaking into a house with intent to steal."

The robbery and minor stabbings were of little interest to the audience, but all eyes turned to Henri Tremblay, the man accused of "the most serious offence in the eyes of God or man." He stared straight ahead, as if he hadn't heard the judge.

Judge Crease continued. "In spite of the fact that there are several cases to be dealt with, there is honour and some satisfaction that the parties accused in every case but one are Chinese, a race that has not yet apparently acquired a proper respect for our laws. These cases will be tried later. As for the present case, Mr. Walkem, I understand you will be representing the interests of the accused, Mr. Henri Tremblay?"

Mr. Walkem rose and bowed. "Yes, My Lord, I appear for the defence."

"Very good. And Mr. Robertson, you'll present the Crown's case against the accused?"

A short blond man stood. He was very young, and his robes were too long. They hung to the floor and covered his boots. "Yes, My Lord."

"Very well. Mr. Robertson, please call your first witness."

"My Lord, there has been an unfortunate development. Two of the witnesses the Crown had hoped to call to testify are unavailable."

"Unavailable to appear before the Supreme Court? That is

not acceptable, Mr. Robertson. Please explain yourself."

The lawyer seemed ill at ease. He shifted his weight from one foot to the other. "My Lord, three Chinese men were summoned as witnesses. One can't be found and another is ill, or claims to be. In truth, when I saw him he bore signs of having been in a most grievous fight. His mouth is badly bruised, and he appears to be missing some teeth. In all honesty I don't believe he could speak clearly enough so that this court could understand his words."

"Very well. He is excused. But the other witness? What do you mean he can't be found?"

"Chief Constable Lindsay has searched for him, My Lord. He...uh...he appears to have left Barkerville, and no one knows where he's gone."

The judge frowned. "As I said in my opening remarks, these Chinese have no respect for our laws. I am not pleased, Mr. Robertson, but in the interests of expediency, I suggest we proceed. Call your remaining witness."

"The witness Ah Ohn is present, My Lord," Mr. Robertson said. "I call Mr. Ohn."

Chief Constable Lindsay disappeared into a door at the back of the courtroom and returned with a tall Chinese man. The court clerk offered Ah Ohn a small piece of paper covered with Chinese writing. The witness struck a match to the corner of it and bowed his head while it burned. He dropped the last piece to the floor, where the clerk hastily stamped on it, making sure the flames were out.

"My Lord, the witness has been sworn according to his beliefs," Mr. Robertson said.

"Very good. Proceed," the judge said absently. His attention was on the black scorch mark on the floor of the courthouse. He didn't look pleased.

"Mr. Ohn, do you require the services of a translator?" Mr. Robertson asked.

"No. I speak English."

"Very good. Then will you tell this court what you saw the morning of November 3 in the year of Our Lord 1870?"

"I saw Ah Mow."

"Yes?"

"He dead."

"Who else did you see?"

"I see white man."

"Could you please tell the court *everything* you saw, Mr. Ohn? Just as you told the coroner at the inquest?"

"I see Ah Mow dead."

"At the inquest you testified that a white man was kneeling beside the body of the deceased. Would you please repeat that statement."

The witness was silent for a moment. Finally he spoke. "Not kneel. No."

"But, Mr. Ohn, you told me that—" Mr. Robertson almost squealed.

He was interrupted by the witness. "I hear Ah Mow shout, 'Murder.' I see Ah Mow dead. I go fetch constable."

The young lawyer was moving his weight from one foot to the other and back. The motion made his robes flap around his boots, sweep across the floor, and stir up small puffs of dust. He coughed, and his voice was lower when he said, "Now, Mr. Ohn, I'll show you a drawing of Barkerville's main street. Uh, does the court clerk have that map?" Mr. Robertson glanced anxiously at the clerk, who rummaged around on his desk for a few seconds before he found a large piece of paper. He handed it to the lawyer and even from the back of the courthouse I could hear Mr. Robertson's sigh of relief. "Thank you. Now, Mr. Ohn, please look at this drawing. It shows Barkerville's main street. Right here is Ah Mow's restaurant." He pointed, and the Chinese man nodded. "And here, where this X is, that's where the deceased was lying. Do you understand?" Again Ah Ohn nodded, and once more the lawyer sighed with relief. "Good. Now will you show me exactly where you were standing?"

The witness studied the map, then reached out a hand and pointed. "Here."

"*There?* Are you sure?"

"Yes. I am in alley."

"In the *alley?* What alley?"

Again the witness pointed at the map.

Mr. Robertson's mouth fell open. He snatched the map out of Ah Ohn's hands and stared at it. "Do you mean this small passageway between two buildings across the street from where the deceased was lying?"

"Yes."

"But at the inquest you testified you were in the street only nine or ten feet from Mr. Mow. This alley is much farther away, perhaps thirty feet."

The witness said nothing. Judge Crease leaned across the bench, craning his neck to see the map, but Mr. Robertson didn't notice.

"You were in the *alley?*" The lawyer's voice had been climbing higher with each question; now it was a high-pitched squeal again. "In the *alley?* You weren't on the street?"

Mr. Robertson was almost bouncing as he shuffled his weight from one foot to the other. I hoped he wouldn't trip over his own robes, but if he didn't stay still, it seemed likely he would end up sprawled on the wooden floor amid the dust he was raising.

"My Lord," Mr. Robertson said to the judge, "I don't understand. This witness has—"

"Just a moment, Mr. Robertson," Judge Crease said. "Mr. Ohn, you do understand you are under oath? You realize there are severe penalties for lying to the Supreme Court?"

"I tell truth," Ah Ohn said.

"But, My Lord, this isn't what he said—"

"It hard to see good in alley," Ah Ohn broke in. "I saw nothing."

Those words! That was exactly what Henri Tremblay had said to me when we met on the Richfield road. *Remember, you saw nothing.*

Last November at the inquest Ah Ohn had sworn he had been only ten feet from the murdered man. He had said he had seen Henri Tremblay kneeling by the body, seen a knife in his hand.

What had happened? Why had Ah Ohn changed his story?

Mr. Robertson had stopped bouncing, and the dust around his feet had settled. He moved to stand directly in front of the witness and tried to lower his voice as he spoke. "Very well then. For now we'll leave the question of exactly where you were standing. Was the white man you saw holding a knife?"

"No knife."

"*What?* I mean, would you repeat that answer."

"I see no knife."

"But at the inquest you said..." Mr. Robertson started bouncing again. "You even identified the type of knife you saw."

"I tell you, no knife. I go now?" Ah Ohn stood, eager to leave.

"Sit down!" Mr. Robertson shouted. "Stay there." Then he turned to the judge. "My Lord?"

"If you're asking me what to do, Mr. Robertson, you're the Crown counsel and I don't consider it part of my duties to conduct this case for you, however young and inexperienced you may be. Perhaps a translator would help, though. Maybe this man's command of English isn't as great as he believes it is and he doesn't understand the questions."

"But he understood perfectly when I interviewed him yesterday, My Lord."

Judge Crease released a deep, impatient sigh. "Do as you wish, Mr. Robertson, but move on. As I said at the beginning, the court has a full schedule and we mustn't delay proceedings simply because you have a reluctant witness."

Mr. Robertson turned to Sing Kee. "Mr. Kee, if you would be so good as to help the court, it would be appreciated."

"I will translate," Sing Kee said, moving to stand beside Ah Ohn's chair. "But there is no need. He understands."

Mr. Robertson cleared his throat, shuffled, and asked, "Did you see a white man with a knife in his hand kneeling beside Ah Mow's body?"

Sing Kee spoke rapidly in Cantonese, and Ah Ohn answered in the same language. The herbalist moved closer to the witness and spoke to him again, this time in a lower voice.

Ah Ohn replied, but he wouldn't look at Sing Kee as he

spoke. His voice was loud, and he used his hands to emphasize whatever he was saying, waving them around and finally thumping a fist on the arm of his chair.

Again Sing Kee spoke. Although he seemed calm, I thought he was becoming angry. His voice was harsh and he bent forward to peer into the witnesses's face as he spoke to him. This time Ah Ohn didn't answer. Instead he shook his head.

"What did the witness say?" Judge Crease demanded. "We don't have all day to listen to this gibberish."

Sing Kee answered the judge in English. "This man says he saw no knife. He says he was in the alley, far away, not close to Ah Mow. He says the white man was standing, not kneeling. I do not believe he tells the truth, but that is what he says."

"Is true," Ah Ohn said. "No knife. No kneel."

In the prisoner's box Henri Tremblay grinned. I don't think anyone but me saw it. He caught me staring at him, and his smirk grew broader.

"Is this the truth?" the judge asked Ah Ohn.

The witness nodded. "Yes. The truth."

"The truth? You do *not* tell the truth," Sing Kee said. Then he switched to rapid Cantonese and shouted a great deal more.

As Ah Ohn listened, his face darkened. He sprang up, knocking his chair over as he pushed it back. Then he took a step toward Sing Kee and began yelling at the herbalist.

Judge Crease got to his feet. He leaned over his bench, banged his gavel, and cried, "Order, order!"

The clerk, too, jumped up and nervously edged away from

his desk, moving a safe distance from the two angry men. Several spectators also rose, anxious for a better view.

Suddenly Chief Constable Lindsay appeared at the front of the courtroom. "Enough of that now. Show some respect, you heathens." One large hand swept down and picked up the overturned chair, setting it upright, while the other hand clamped firmly on Ah Ohn's shoulder and forced the witness back into the chair. Meanwhile Sing Kee returned to his place with the other witnesses.

The court clerk cautiously went back to his desk, but Judge Crease continued to lean across the bench, banging the gavel. "Order. There will be no more shouting. There *will* be order in this court. Be seated at once."

The spectators who were still on their feet sat down again. After the clerk slid into his chair and picked up his pen, Judge Crease sat and adjusted his wig, which had slipped slightly as he had wielded the gavel.

By now *both* lawyers were on their feet. Mr. Walkem strode toward the judge's bench, his black robes billowing around him, appearing even more like the large, hungry raven I had thought he resembled the day of the inquest. "My Lord, this is shameful behaviour in—"

"I am quite aware of what is happening in *my* court, Mr. Walkem," Judge Crease snapped. "Return to your seat."

"Very well, My Lord," Mr. Walkem said, doing as he was told.

Mr. Robertson remained alone in the centre of the room, shuffling back and forth. He looked as if he were about to cry, but he inhaled deeply, turned to Ah Ohn, and said as sternly as he could, "Sir, for the last time, did you see a white man with a knife in his hand kneeling beside the body of Ah Mow?"

"No. No knife. No kneel."

"But you did see Mr. Tremblay, didn't you?" the lawyer asked.

"Mr. Robertson, that is not an appropriate question at this point, as you know full well," Judge Crease said. "Please respect the—"

"Maybe not same white man," Ah Ohn said. "Maybe different. Hard to see."

"Are you saying that you no longer recognize the defendant as the man you saw the morning of the murder?" Mr. Robertson asked. Everyone in the courtroom could hear the desperation in his voice.

Mr. Walkem was on his feet again, bearing down on the bench, but Judge Crease motioned him back. "Sit down, Mr. Walkem. I think we need to hear this answer no matter how inappropriate the question.

Ah Ohn glanced briefly at Henri Tremblay before he replied. "Different white man." He pointed at the prisoner's box. "Different. He not in street with Ah Mow."

"But that's not true!" The voice came from someone in the second to last row of the crowded courtroom. "He's not telling the truth."

The judge thumped his gavel hard, and Pa grabbed my elbow. "Be still, son. Sit down and be quiet."

I realized I was standing and that every pair of eyes in the courtroom was fixed on me, including the judge's stern ones, Mr. Robertson's hopeful ones, and Henri Tremblay's cold ones.

"I can't be quiet, Pa," I whispered. "That man is lying. Someone has to tell the truth. I was there. I saw—"

"You must sit down," my father said sternly, pulling on my arm. "This is none of your concern."

"Young man," asked the judge, "how do you explain this outburst? Have you been called as a witness?"

"No, My Lord."

"Then please be seated. I will excuse your disrespect this once, due to your youth, but any further attempt on your part to interrupt the court proceedings will be dealt with harshly. Sit down and let us continue with the trial."

"No! I mean, My Lord, I was there... Pa, leave me alone. Let me speak."

My father held on to my arm tightly, trying to pull me back into my seat.

"Sit down, young man," Judge Crease said firmly.

"No," I said again loudly, and this time the judge heard me.

"Pardon me?" he said, eyebrows rising in astonishment until they almost met the edge of his wig. "Did you say no? Did I just hear you refuse a request of mine in my own court-room?" He scowled.

"I have to speak," I said. "I have to tell you..."

And then, though my mouth kept moving, nothing came out of it except a thin, whistling squeak. I gulped, wincing against the pain in my throat, and tried once more, but again there was no sound.

My father was no longer trying to make me sit. Now he stood close beside me, nudging me none too gently, trying to get me to move past the people seated beside us.

"My son isn't well, My Lord," he said. "He has a fever. Please allow me to take him home."

The judge was silent for a moment, then his scowl faded

143

and he nodded. "I understand how the excitement of these proceedings could have aggravated the boy's condition. Take him away."

"No," I said again as forcefully as I could. "You must listen to me. I was there. I saw both of them, Mr. Tremblay and—"

"Excuse us, please, thank you." Although my voice was softer than a newborn kitten's mewling, my father was taking no chances on my being heard. He talked loudly as he pushed me along. "Excuse us, the lad's ill. He doesn't know what he's saying."

"I *do* know what I'm saying." No one heard me. My voice had completely gone and not even a kitten's squeak emerged from my mouth. I dug my heels into the floor and tried to stand my ground, but my father was stronger and heavier than I. In spite of my efforts to remain where I was, he succeeded in steering me past the last person on the bench and into the aisle.

"Shall I help you remove your son from the courtroom, Mr. MacIntosh?" Chief Constable Lindsay looked as if he would be eager to help Pa, that he would enjoy a chance to shove me out the door.

"Nae, thank you, Constable. We'll leave quietly, won't we, son?"

I shook my head and opened my mouth again, but Pa was right. I had no choice but to leave quietly, for I could say nothing that anyone could hear.

The chief constable swung open the door and ushered us out. "Some youngsters should learn to keep their opinions to themselves. There's no need to make more trouble for poor Mr. Tremblay. As I said before, Mr. MacIntosh, a trip to the woodshed for your headstrong boy would teach him to keep his mouth shut."

"But—" I said again, or tried to say.

"Thank you for your advice, Constable," my father said. "Although I nae believe in beating a child, be assured I shall speak severely to Ted."

The chief constable seemed disappointed as he shut the door behind us. I had a strong suspicion he wouldn't mind giving me that whipping himself.

Sixteen

Neither Pa nor I said anything on the way home. I was silent because I still couldn't speak. Pa said nothing because he was angry at me. We walked past the group of Chinese men, and I saw Peter's anxious face. When Peter tried to talk to me, my father said, "Not now. The lad is sick."

After we arrived at our house, my mother looked at us questioningly. But all Pa said was: "He's ill. Put him to bed and keep him here. I'm going back to the trial." Then he turned and left.

My mother ushered me into bed and, against my feeble protests, fed me the rest of the cough medicine and closed my bedroom door firmly. "Stay there," she said.

I protested again, but not too much. I didn't feel well. My head throbbed and my throat pained me so greatly I could barely swallow. I lay down and fell asleep.

As I slept, I dreamed. Once I thought Henri Tremblay stood by my bedside, telling me to get up and fight like a man. "No," I told him, "I'm not a man, not yet." I screamed, or tried to.

Suddenly Ma was beside me, a damp towel in her hands.

She sat on the edge of the bed and bathed my face, talking to me gently. "There's no one here, son. No one but me and your father. Rest and try not to think about..."

She didn't say what I shouldn't think about, but it didn't matter. I fell asleep again, and the dreams continued.

Jenny. Peter. Ah Mow, the blood streaming from his chest. Judge Crease leaning over my bed, pounding his gavel on my forehead. Jenny again. Then Henri Tremblay once more, this time stabbing a knife into my throat over and over, telling me, "You will say nothing. You know nothing."

Then Jenny again, sitting beside me, crying. Peter once more, pulling on my arm, urging me to get up and race with him. Again, Jenny, this time holding a cold cloth to my forehead, whispering to me, followed by Chief Constable Lindsay, a leather strap in his hand, ordering me to come with him to the woodshed. Then Sing Kee, holding my head and gently urging me to take a sip of medicine. Then Jenny sitting beside me, whispering, "You're a glaikit boy to take so ill. Please get well."

There had been so many people in my bedroom that I was surprised when I opened my eyes and saw only my mother and father. "Where is everyone?" I asked.

"Oh, Ted, you can speak."

"Of course I can speak, Ma," I croaked, my voice as husky as a raven's.

"I'm glad to hear your voice, son," my father said. He seemed tired, as if he hadn't had much sleep, but he smiled when he spoke again. "Very glad."

"I don't understand."

"You haven't said a word for three days, not to me or even

to your mother, though once you screamed."

"Three days?" I said. "What do you mean? We left the trial this morning and came home and then—"

"We put you to bed and you've been here ever since, the fever raging through you. Your mother has scarcely left your side."

"Three days?" I repeated. "But how—"

"Hush, don't try to talk," Ma said. She was sitting on the bed beside me, pressing a damp cloth against my forehead.

I pushed her hand away. "Three days? That can't be possible."

"It is," Pa said. "You've been very ill."

"Dr. Bell has been to see you," my mother said. "Sing Kee, too. I think it was his medicine, not the doctor's, that finally broke your fever." She handed me a glass of water. "Take only small sips. You must drink as much as you can, but slowly, for nothing but a few drops of water has passed your lips in all this time. Sip slowly, then lie down again."

"But the trial! I have to go back."

"The trial is over," Pa said.

"Over? The hanging, too?"

My parents looked at each other. "There's no need to think of that right now," my father said.

"Don't worry about it," my mother urged. "Lie back down and rest."

"I must know! Ma? Pa? Tell me! Has it happened?"

"Ted, try not to—" Ma began.

"It isn't important," Pa broke in.

"Tell me! Please."

Again my parents exchanged glances. Then my mother stood. "He won't rest until he knows. You'd best tell him,

Ian. I'll go and make some broth. Perhaps he can take a bit of nourishment." She left the room.

"Pa? Tell me the truth. Is Mr. Tremblay dead? Has he been executed?"

"There was no hanging, Ted, nor will there be one. The jury found Tremblay not guilty. He's a free man."

"Not guilty! That's impossible."

"Aye, that's more or less what Judge Crease thought. He told the jury he didn't agree with its decision."

"So why didn't he make the jury change the verdict?"

"A judge can't do that. A jury's decision is final. Not even a judge can alter it. However, Judge Crease told Tremblay that he had escaped punishment by the skin of his teeth."

"By the skin of his teeth?"

"Aye. But your mother is right. Now isn't the time for you to worry about that. When you're well enough, you can read everything that happened, for the newspaper has been full of nothing else. Now lie back down and rest."

I did as he said, and once more I slept.

My mother woke me, how much later I didn't know. She propped my head up with pillows, then sat beside me. "Open your mouth. I've made a fresh broth. You must eat."

"I can feed myself," I said, struggling to push away the spoon.

Ma paid no attention. She thrust a spoonful of soup at me, and I obediently opened my mouth. My throat didn't hurt when I swallowed, and I suddenly realized I was very hungry.

"Please, Ma, give it to me."

She shook her head and spooned out more. I felt like a small child again, or a baby bird, opening my mouth, swallowing, opening it again. But I was too hungry to object. I just wanted to eat.

The bowl was nearly empty, when there was a noise outside the bedroom door and Jenny burst in, followed by my father. "She wouldn't wait until we could make the lad respectable," he said. "I told her he would want to be tidied before he saw her, but she wouldn't listen."

"Ted! Oh, you glaikit boy. How could you get so ill? I've been here every day, and you couldn't sit up or speak and I thought you were dying. You've made me worry so much that..." Then she burst into tears.

"He'll recover, Miss Jenny," my father said. "Don't cry."

My mother stood and put down the bowl of soup and the spoon. She was crying, too. "Yes, he's better, Jenny."

"Jenny," I said, "you're here!"

"Did I not say I've been here every day?" Although there were still tears streaming down her cheeks, she smiled. "Did you nae hear a word I said?"

"I thought I was dreaming."

"Oh, aye, you were dreaming," Jenny said. "You tossed and turned and the sweat poured from your brow and you were so hot I like to have burned my fingers when I touched your face."

"I'm sorry I was sick," I said, embarrassed. "But I'm well now. Why are you crying?"

"Because I'm so happy you are well at last," she said. "For you to get sick, that was nae the right thing to do, not just after you kissed me. It wasn't a...a gentlemanly way to behave at all. It was very unmannerly of you. I shall never let you kiss me again if you get ill every time I do so."

"Uh...Jenny..." I tried to stop her from saying anything else, but it was no use.

Ma moved closer to my bed, and I could tell that both she and Pa were listening carefully. Pa was grinning, but Ma didn't seem pleased.

"Jenny..." I tried again, but Jenny went right on talking.

"First you won't race with me, then you hold my hand and kiss me, then you get ill, and even though I brought you shortbreads and sat by your bedside every day, not once did you say my name. Not once."

"Jenny," I said. "Jenny, Jenny, Jenny. I say it now."

"Oh," she said, sitting on the bed beside me, reaching out and taking my hand. "Oh, Ted."

My father coughed, and she quickly pulled her hand back.

"You mustn't stay long, Miss Jenny," my mother said. "Ted is still weak, and he needs to take more nourishment. Then he must rest."

"I shall not tire him, Mrs. MacIntosh. But, oh, to see him sitting up and speaking when I thought I should never see him again except as a cold corpse laid out in his best suit for his funeral. He would have been shaved, of course. Not all scratchy looking as he is now."

"Corpse?" I said. "Was I really that ill?"

"Yes, you were, and I shall never forgive you for it," Jenny said seriously.

"You were here?" I asked. "It wasn't a dream?"

"Nae, it was not. I was here every day, sometimes two or three times a day." She reached out to take my hand again, but this time it was my mother who coughed a warning, and Jenny folded her hands demurely and put them in her lap.

"Now that you've reassured yourself that Ted is mending, it's time you returned to Barkerville, Jenny," Ma said firmly. "You may come back tomorrow, or as soon as Ted is on his feet once more. The bedroom is not a suitable place for you to visit him."

"Or to do your courting," my father said equally firmly.

"I'm sorry," Jenny said, but she made no move to leave. She smiled at me again, and I realized there wasn't a trace of the bootblack moustache left on her face.

"Please, Ma, let her stay a while longer. I feel much stronger."

"No, not today," my mother said.

"Pa?"

"Your mother knows what's best for you, son."

"Very well, I shall go," Jenny said. "But I'll come back."

"Yes," Ma said. "I've no doubt you will."

"He'll want to know all about the trial," Pa said. "Perhaps you can come tomorrow, Miss Jenny, and read to him from the paper, if he's still too weak to read for himself."

"Oh, what matters all of that?" Jenny said. "He's well again. That's what matters."

"It's over, Jenny," I said. I was thinking of Ah Mow's death, of the angry Chinese men in Sing Kee's shop, of Henri Tremblay smirking from the prisoner's box, of Ah Ohn saying, *Maybe different white man.* "It's over."

But Jenny wasn't thinking about any of that.

"Over?" She seemed surprised. Even though Ma and Pa glared at her, she took my hand in hers, held it for a long moment, and smiled at me. "Oh, you glaikit boy, it is nae over. It's only just beginning."

Afterword

Ah Mow was killed in November 1870, and my information about that murder and the testimony at the inquest and trial comes from newpaper reports and court records. Because the real defendant was found not guilty, and also because I needed a villain in this story, I chose not to use the historical person involved but to invent the fictitious Henri Tremblay instead. Many witnesses did substantially change their testimony between the inquest and the trial. I have suggested they were threatened and made to do so, but there is no historical evidence to support that theory. However, prejudice against the Chinese was so strong at the time that I suspect the all-white jury wouldn't have found a fellow white man guilty no matter what evidence was presented. The judge made public his disapproval of the verdict when he stated that, in his opinion, the defendant had escaped punishment "by the skin of his teeth."

Theodore Percival MacIntosh, better known as Ted, is also fictional, as are his family, Bridget, Jenny, and Peter. Ted appears first in *Moses, Me and Murder: A Story of the Cariboo Gold Rush* (Pacific Educational Press, 1988) and continues his adventures in *The Doctor's Apprentice* (Beach Holme Publishing, 1998).

ANN WALSH is the author of *Your Time, My Time, Shabash!*, and *The Ghost of Soda Creek* (a Canadian Library Association's Notable Selection). She is also the creator of the Barkerville historical mystery series, whose first two novels are *Moses, Me and Murder* and *The Doctor's Apprentice* (nominated for the Sheila Egoff Award for Children's Literature). As an editor, she has published two anthologies of children's stories, *Winds Through Time* and *Beginnings*. All her books have received the Canadian Children's Book Centre Our Choice Award, and she has also earned nominations for the Silver Birch and Geoffrey Bilson Awards. She lives in Williams Lake, British Columbia.